Mask Appeal

Read all the Cinderella Cleaners books!

MAYA GOLD

SCHOLASTIC INC.

New York   Toronto   London   Auckland
Sydney   Mexico City   New Delhi   Hong Kong

For Emily, with Hugs & Kisses

ISBN 978-0-545-12962-6

12 11 10 9 8 7 6 5 4 3 2 1   10 11 12 13 14 15/0

Printed in the U.S.A.   40
First edition, August 2010

Book design by Yaffa Jaskoll

Chapter One

It's half an hour since my alarm clock went off, and I'm fully dressed except for my feet.

I've settled on fuzzy striped socks, but I'm having an indecision attack over my shoelaces. I can't remember exactly when I started mix-and-matching the laces on my Converses, but it's become my trademark look, and I change the color combo at least once a week. I keep a rainbow of different colored laces in a basket on top of my bureau.

"Diana!" my stepmother, Fay, yells up the staircase. "You're going to be late!"

"Coming!" I answer, and squeeze my eyes shut as I plunge my hand into the basket. Sometimes a random pick is the best way to go.

1

I grab two laces and open my eyes. Orange in one hand, black and white checks in the other. Well, why not? It *is* almost Halloween.

I sit on the edge of my bed and thread in the new laces. The black and white checks look a little insane with the striped socks, so how about . . . purple? Orange and purple. No, purple and *turquoise*.

So much for the random pick. The thing is, I really love fashion, and detail is everything. A cool pair of earrings, the way a scarf drapes, or the right choice of belt can make all the difference. It's about how you *feel* in the outfit you're wearing. When I'm in a play at school, my costume is mega important. When you put on a character's shoes, you put on her walk. You become someone else for a while.

I love that.

Not that I've gotten to be in a play this fall. This is the year Fay decided I needed to help out after school at Dad's dry-cleaning business, Cinderella Cleaners, so I had to drop out of Drama Club for the time being. I thought I would mind, but the job has turned out to be more fun than I ever could have imagined. Among other things, I'm surrounded by clothes every afternoon. Which totally rocks.

My two-tone Converse high-tops look great with my socks, favorite jeans, and teal green V-neck sweater. I bounce past my twin stepsisters' room, where they're having their usual fight about who stole whose barrette. Their voices spill into the hall.

"I did *not* take it off of your dresser!" That's Brynna, the whiner.

"Then who did?" That's Ashley, the boss.

"I don't *know*!" Brynna whimpers.

It's tough to be nine.

I head down to the kitchen to make my school lunch. Today's a no-brainer. Fay had to work late at her real estate office last night, so after Dad closed up at the cleaners, he and I picked up a couple of pizzas from Benny's. The twins and Fay ate up all the Extra Cheese, but there are two slices left of the Broccoli-Garlic-and-Mushroom, and my favorite lunch in the world is cold pizza. I lay one slice on top of the other, face-to-face like a giant triangular sandwich, and reach for the foil. Fay is frowning.

"You call that a lunch?" She's just spread grape jelly and Skippy on white bread for Ashley and Brynna, so if we're going to butt heads about good nutrition, I think possibly

3

broccoli wins. But I've promised my dad I'll be nicer to Fay, and he's sitting right there at the table, so I just smile and reach for the carrot sticks.

"Want me to pack some of these for the girls?" I ask, and she nods. Would it kill her to say "Thank you"? I toss carrots into three ziplock bags, grab an orange and a juice box for my lunch, and I'm good to go.

"Bye, Dad," I say, leaning over to kiss him on top of his head. He looks up from his newspaper, raising his eyebrows. They're dark like mine, though everyone tells me I look much more like my mother. I wish that were true. I got her wavy brown hair and brown eyes — Dad's are blue — but not the irresistible twinkle that makes me miss her bright smile every morning.

"You're not eating breakfast?" Dad asks. I hold up a granola bar, and he makes a face. "More than one food group, please."

Are he and Fay in this together? "It has dried fruit and nuts," I say, rolling my eyes. "And I'm having orange juice, see?"

"How about some eggs?" Fay pipes up, and I'm trapped.

• • •

4

Two fried eggs and a piece of toast later, I'm barreling out the door to meet up with my best friend, Jess Munson, who lives two blocks away. The fact that I'm late doesn't mean much, since she's always later. Jess's mom is the queen of last minute.

We meet at the corner — me tearing up my street with my scarf flapping wildly, Jess streaking down hers with her jacket unzipped in spite of the chill in the air.

"Beat you!" yells Jess, though she didn't, not really.

"Fay fed me fried eggs," I explain.

Jess *hates* fried eggs, especially when the yolks are runny. She shudders, her red curls tossing under her signature Mad Hatter top hat. "Ugh. Better you than me."

We turn onto Underhill Avenue, heading up the long hill toward Weehawken Middle School. My next-door neighbor, Mr. Wheeler, crosses the street with his two tiny papillon dogs jumping up and down on their leashes. Jess always calls them "the yappers," but I think they're cute. I love the way their ears stand straight up, like bows on a hat.

My eyes follow them as Mr. Wheeler walks past the Underhill Deli, and I spot a new poster in the front window. The poster is bright orange, with a graphic of eyes peering through a black satin mask. I look up the street and notice the same poster's stapled to every phone pole. Before I have time to react, Jess is pointing to one.

"What's with the mask?" she asks. "Is someone doing *Phantom*?"

"Not without *us*," I respond, since *Phantom of the Opera* is on my all-time Top Ten list of Broadway shows. There's nothing quite as romantic as a mysterious guy in a mask. When I was little, my favorite DVDs were *The Princess Bride* and *Zorro*.

We move closer to look at the poster, which reads:

Dance with the Stars at
Hunger Unmasked

"Oh, of course. It's that fund-raiser thing they do every year," Jess says.

I nod. "I heard last year's was great." We keep reading eagerly.

Masquerade Ball to Benefit Arts Against Hunger
• Live Music by Dreamcatcher

- Silent Art Auction
- Fleet Feet Dancers
- PLUS Broadway Stars from *Bye Bye Birdie* and —

I gasp out loud. *"Angel!"*

Angel is a new Broadway musical starring my major celebrity crush, Adam Kessler. I used to have a Zac Efron photo as my desktop background, and now it's Adam instead, so we're talking *incredibly* cute.

When I first started helping out at the cleaners, I found a pair of tickets to *Angel*'s opening night that had been left behind by a customer. By a series of chances that still feels like magic, I went to the show's opening night and got to meet Adam, who's even dreamier in person. Then Jess won a raffle and got to see the show, too. Which is now on our all-time Top *One* list.

I wonder what "stars" will be at this masquerade ball. Could one be . . . *him*?

As usual, Jess is right on my wavelength. "Do you think Adam Kessler —?" we say at exactly the same time.

Jess laughs and tags my arm. "You owe me a Coke," she says, which we started saying in nursery school.

"No, you owe *me* a Coke," I reply, while my heart does a little flip-flop at the thought of seeing Adam in person again.

Not that either Jess or I can afford to attend the ball — according to the poster, the tickets cost eighty dollars apiece, with a discount of one hundred fifty dollars per couple. It's all for a good cause, of course, but those aren't eighth-grade prices.

"Don't you wish . . ." I start, and Jess says, "Yes!" before I even finish my sentence.

"It just looks so *glamorous*," I go on dreamily.

Jess nods. "I wish I could bring Jason."

Jason Geissinger is Jess's new crush — I might almost have to say *boyfriend* — who goes to the Foreman Academy, a snooty prep school where Jess and I went to a dance and had some adventures. They've seen each other exactly twice since, but they're setting world records for texting. Whenever Jess mentions his name, which is all the time, I know I'm going to be in for a monologue. But before she can really get going now, a gust of wind picks up her top hat, blowing it into a nearby hedge.

Something else blows past us, too — a loose poster from the next phone pole. I want that!

We pounce like two kittens. Jess scoops up her hat and I grab the poster, and we're both so excited we charge to the top of the hill. Our gym teacher would be proud.

We're just turning into the school parking lot, still breathing hard, when a long line of empty yellow buses starts to move down the driveway. We really *are* late.

"Uh-oh," I say, and we pour on the speed, skidding through the front doors just before the first bell rings for homeroom.

It's not till I go back to my locker for lunch that I remember the Hunger Unmasked poster I saved from the wind. (Maybe the eight by ten photo of Adam Kessler inside my locker door, wedged between Robert Pattinson and Johnny Depp, is the reminder.) I take the poster out and look at the mask again. I can practically hear the rustle of silk and see elegant dancers swirling in pairs. *Will* Adam be one of the guest Broadway stars? I would so love to go!

Will Carson stops by on the way to his locker. He's

wearing his usual band logo T-shirt — Modest Mouse, whose name seems to suit his don't-look-at-me bangs and shy manner.

"What's that?" he says, looking over my shoulder. I show him the poster, feeling suddenly super self-conscious. Will and I like each other, more than a little and maybe a lot, which makes things that used to be normal feel totally awkward. Like having those fan photos inside my locker. Or being aware that he's standing so close and is just the right inch or two taller than me.

Am I blushing? I hope not.

"This looks mad cool," says Will, scanning the poster. "I've heard of this Dreamcatcher band."

The date is next Friday, I notice — the day before Halloween. I also see there's a Web site, and make a mental note to look it up when I get home.

Will lets out a low whistle. "A hundred and fifty bucks, whoa."

He's pointing at the discount price, the one that's for couples. Will darts a quick look at me, then looks away fast. Great, now we're *both* blushing.

It is *so* much easier crushing on celebrities than a real

guy you actually know. Perfectly innocent words, like "couple" or "talking to," or even something as simple as "with," can blow up in your face.

"Are you going to lunch or the band room?" I ask quickly, tucking the poster on top of my afternoon books.

"Lunch," says Will, mumbling a quick "See you there" before scuttling off to his locker.

See you *there*? Really? I'm going there, too, duh. So couldn't we walk down the staircase together, like we used to before all this liking-each-other stuff got in the way and made everything mean much too much?

Apparently not. Will's bending over his combination lock as if twisting the dial is some kind of brain surgery that needs every ounce of his concentration. I could wait till he's done, but I don't want to stalk the guy, so I grab my lunch bag and go down the stairs by myself.

Am I imagining things, or does Will look after me as soon as my back is turned? This is getting ridiculous. Aren't we just friends, plus a little bit extra?

That "little bit extra" is killer.

• • •

I always eat lunch with the same three friends: Jess, of course, Sara Parvati, and Amelia Williams. Straight-A student Sara and sporty Amelia are each other's besties, just like me and Jess, and the four of us love to hang out as a group. But lately our table has swelled to include Will, Ethan Horowitz, who's been my friend since forever, and — this is the deal breaker — Ethan's girlfriend, Kayleigh Carell.

Kayleigh is that queen-bee blond cheerleader every middle school seems to have, as predictable as the perfume wafting out of a Hollister store (which she wears 24/7, just to make sure we know where she shops). She's the bane of my life, because unlike most cheerleaders, she thinks she's an actress and goes out for Drama Club like me and Jess. Why can't she stick to her own clique? It's just *wrong*.

Kayleigh started eating with us when Sara and I got cast in a music video starring Kayleigh's favorite pop singer, Tasha Kane. This made us at least temporarily cool. But she can't quite decide between kissing up to us and her usual dripping disdain, which makes lunch conversations a little bit weird. You never know which side of Kayleigh you'll get.

Sara starts opening take-out containers from her family's Indian restaurant and wonderful curry smells float through the air. I'm suddenly starving. I take my lunch bag off my pile of books and unwrap my pizza sandwich.

"Trade you a bite for a bite," says Jess, holding up her ham and Swiss. I nod, even though she's put on so much mustard her rye bread looks yellow.

Kayleigh leans over the table, flipping her blond hair away from her face with one hand as she looks at the Hunger Unmasked poster sitting on top of my math book.

"Oh, the *masquerade* ball," she says, putting her other hand on Ethan's arm as if he were a purse she was carrying. "We've got tickets for that, don't we, Ethan?" Sometimes Kayleigh seems to be running her own private contest to see how many times she can use the word *we* in a sentence. Everyone gets it, okay? You're a *couple*. Big whoop.

I look down the table at Will, who's best friends with Ethan and doesn't like Kayleigh much better than I do. He's dredging a buffalo wing through blue cheese dressing. Sometimes his lunch is leftovers from the Craft Services table on video sets. Will's father was the recording engineer on Tasha Kane's video, which is how I got to try out for it, with the help of a really cool vest that I found at the cleaners.

But Kayleigh's not done yet. "My parents already bought tickets for us," she says, smirking at me. "They're really expensive."

"Too bad Diana hasn't been paid for the Tasha Kane video yet," Jess can't resist saying. "She could buy tickets for all of us out of her fee." Kayleigh's lower lip, shiny with gloss, curls into a pout.

Just then Amelia comes back from the hot lunch line with a tray full of popcorn shrimp, wax beans, and corn. Her whole lunch is yellow and tan. So is her outfit — a pale yellow hoodie and khakis. With her blond ponytail and outdoor tan, she looks kind of yellow and tan herself.

"Where'd you get *that*?" she asks, eyeing the poster as she settles down at the end of the table. "My sister's dance school is performing there."

"The Fleet Feet Dancers?" Jess asks her, at the same time as I ask, "What stars are coming from *Angel*?"

"Fleet Feet, right. No idea what stars — if they knew, you can bet it would be on the poster," Amelia says calmly, answering both of our questions at once. She pops a shrimp into her mouth. "Ooh, hot," she says, fanning her mouth with one hand. "My mother is making me volunteer at this thing."

My ears prick up. "Really? Do they need more volunteers?"

"I can ask, but I totally doubt it," Amelia says. "Mom's drafted every kid in Fleet Feet who won't be on the stage. Plus lucky me."

"Hey, if you want to trade places," says Jess, "I'd love to get a free pass to this. So would Diana."

Amelia shakes her head glumly. "No way I can get out of this one. My mom was a dancer when she was young, and it's her whole world. You'd think having one daughter in toe shoes would be enough, but she keeps hoping I'm a late bloomer who'll drop soccer and get into dance if she just keeps *exposing* me to it. Good luck with that, Mom."

"So we'll see you there," Kayleigh says brightly, draping her arm around Ethan's neck as she beams at Amelia. "It'll be so *fun!*"

I'm sorry, but there's something wrong with a world where Kayleigh Carell gets to go to a glamorous masquerade ball — possibly with *Adam Kessler* as a special guest — and Jess and I don't.

I must look way disappointed, because Amelia studies my face as she finishes chewing her shrimp. Then she says, "Let me talk to my mom," in a voice that sounds more like, "We'll work something out."

Yes!

Chapter Two

Jess and I don't see Amelia again till last period, when she catches up to us in the hallway outside geometry class.

"So here's what I'm thinking," she says, looking over her shoulder to make sure that no one's in earshot. "There's no way to get you in as volunteers — they've already assigned us costumes."

"Really?" I say. That sounds awesome! How can Amelia not want to do it?

"*Ballet* costumes," she says, looking sour. "Don't get me started. But I can sign up to work at the door, taking tickets or something, and I'll figure out some way to sneak you guys in."

"That would be amazing!" I tell her. "But I don't want to get you in trouble."

"It'll be fine," says Amelia. "I'll be super careful."

I'm excited, but not convinced. "What if they need you to work somewhere else?"

Amelia shrugs. "I'll tell my mom I want to be next to the door so I can watch Zoe dance. It'll make her day, trust me."

"Can I invite Jason?" Jess asks, and I practically step on her foot. Isn't sneaking in two of us enough of a favor to ask? But Amelia's not fazed.

"Why not?" she says. "Most people show up in pairs, so you'd fit right in."

Jess turns to me. "You should bring Will!" she says, and I blush the color of ketchup. Will and I aren't a "pair"! What's the matter with her? But before I can speak, or sputter, our math teacher, Mr. Perotta, comes out of the classroom.

"The bell has *rung*, ladies," he says with a unibrow frown.

"Coming!" says Amelia, and we file through the door under his outstretched arm. As we're taking our seats in the back of the classroom, Jess turns to Amelia, whispering one last question. "Won't your mom recognize us if you sneak us in?"

"Hello, it's a *masquerade* ball," says Amelia. "Figure it out."

Now I'm back in my comfort zone. I smile and tell Jess, "Leave that part to me." Finding the right outfit is never a problem — after all, I have an after-school job in the world's largest costume shop! With a little imagination, Cinderella Cleaners always has something that's *perfect*. You might even say tailor-made.

The masquerade ball is all I can think about as I'm riding the school bus to work. I see posters for Hunger Unmasked all over the place, and sure enough, when I get to the cleaners, there's one right in the window. I'm not supposed to go in the front door, but I can't resist going to look at that mask one more time. As I stand there and stare at it, somebody raps on the glass. I jump back with a guilty start. It's my supervisor, Miss MacInerny, her lips pulled together in a tight frown as she points toward the employee entrance.

Is she for real? I'm reading a *poster*. I glance at the customer counter behind her to see if my friend Catalina is working the cash register. Cat would think this was a riot — I can imagine her rolling her eyes. But instead it's the new trainee, Lara Nekrasova, and the expression she has on her face is a virtual mirror of our cranky boss's. Are there *two* of them now?

I mouth "Sorry" at Miss MacInerny and scamper around to the back door, where I pull on my green smock, pin on my name tag, and stash my things inside my locker in record time, trying to prove I'm a model employee in spite of the dread poster-reading offense. Cat and I like to call MacInerny "Joyless" (her first name is, ironically, Joy), but I still can't believe she'd get mad over something so minor. It's like when a teacher gets in your face about some tiny detail, like whether you printed your name or used cursive on top of a test, and you want to say, "Take a chill pill," but you know it'll just make things worse.

Since MacInerny's on the warpath, I know I should hurry up front to get my first assignment, but I can't resist taking a quick peek at the No Pickup rack. Last time I looked, it included a sparkly pink gown that would be *perfect* for Hunger Unmasked. My fingers are crossed that it hasn't been claimed by the client who left it last month. I wonder how people lose track of their clothes. Did the owner forget that she dropped off her gown for dry cleaning, decide that she couldn't afford it, get dumped by her date, move to Brazil? Anything's possible.

I breathe a sigh of relief when I see the pink gown is still on the rack, unclaimed. It's even more gorgeous than I remembered, with gold embroidery on the bodice and a full ruffled skirt. It would be totally perfect with a cute mask. I look at the tag, and my heart sinks when I see it's two sizes too big for me.

My buddy Nelson Martinez would know how to fix it — Nelson's the head tailor, and he can fix anything — but he's been on a leave of absence for weeks now. He had a sensational top secret job working for Tasha Kane's costume designer, and I'm starting to worry that he won't ever come back.

I put the pink gown back on the rack and hurry through the workroom, passing the giant steam presser, the noisy

21

dry-cleaning machines, and the work table where Rose Chen is spot-cleaning rugs, wearing goggles and gloves like a chemist. I push through the big double doors to the customer counter, which is sunlit and pleasant, a whole different world. MacInerny is handing a bald man with glasses a group of pressed button-down shirts, all pale blue, like the one he's wearing today with his gray suit and navy tie. If I had to wear the same thing every day, I'd go out of my mind.

Lara rings him up on the cash register. She's been working here longer than I have, but she's just been promoted to customer service to fill in for my friend Elise, who plays varsity basketball at Hoboken High School and won't be around till the basketball season is over.

Lara is Russian. She has a musical accent and a face that reminds me a bit of a fox, with slanting green eyes and sharp cheekbones. She's in her twenties, but wears her hair pulled up in a tight bun that makes her look older. She hands the customer change, then turns toward me, saying, "You're late."

I'm totally taken aback. For one thing, I'm not — it's three-fifteen on the dot. For another, she isn't my boss. Is she trying to gain points with Joyless? If so, imitating her might not be the best way to go. But MacInerny beams like a proud mom whose daughter just won a blue ribbon for Perfect Attendance. It might be the first time I've seen her smile, not counting her fake-friendly smirk at the customers. I make a mental note to tell Cat when she gets in, but Lara's already giving me instructions.

"You vill bring this to Tailorink," she says, turning to hand me a black-and-white checkered coat.

"Will Loretta and Sadie know what to —"

"It is marked," Lara says in a don't-you-know-anything tone, and I notice a chalk circle under one arm, where the fabric has split and the lining is fraying.

"Fine," I say, wondering again why she's being so sharp with me. I'm only a little annoyed, though — the Tailoring section is my favorite place in the cleaners. Especially today, when I open the door and see Nelson grinning at me!

"You're back!" I cry, too happy to care that, duh, that's pretty obvious. The last I heard, Tasha's designer had offered him ongoing work, but I guess it's —

"Part-time," Nelson says, as if he's finishing the sentence in my head. With his angled fedora, popped collar,

23

hipster suspenders, and heavy-soled shoes, he looks like he just walked out of an Urban Outfitters catalog. "What have you got for me?"

I hand him the black-and-white coat, and his eyebrows go up in twin arches. "Somebody's mother had taste," he says. "This is vintage Chanel. Early sixties, I'd say."

"Really?" I wouldn't have guessed it was anything special. There's so much to learn about fashion design.

"Oh, absolutely," says Loretta, one of the two white-haired seamstresses. "That cut is bee-yoo-tiful, isn't it, Sadie?"

Sadie nods. "Truly."

Nelson looks inside the sleeve and frowns. "Some fool repaired this silk lining with cheap polyester. No wonder it's shredding. Is there something else?" He's looking at me with a very slight smile on his lips, like he's already guessed that there is. I glance at Loretta and Sadie, but they're both bent back over their sewing machines. I give a quick nod. Nelson takes my arm, guiding me to the far side of the fabric racks, where we're out of earshot. "So what is it this time?"

"Just a small alteration. A gown on the No Pickup rack."

"Pretty in Pink?" I nod, amazed. Sometimes he really is like a mind reader. "Where do you plan to wear *that*, to an eighties theme party? No, wait, let me guess. Where would you want to wear a pink satin gown? To the Hunger Unmasked Ball."

"Yes!" I say, awestruck. "How did you *know*? Are you going, too?"

"Can't. Much too much on my dance card," says Nelson. "But I'm sewing four costumes for it this weekend. In fact, if you can come in for a few hours on Sunday and help me . . ."

Now it's my turn to finish his thought. ". . . you'll alter my gown?"

"Better yet," Nelson says. "I'll teach *you* how to alter it. Tailoring lessons in trade for your time. Do we have a deal?"

Do we ever! It's all I can do not to throw my arms around Nelson and burst into song. This is going to be great!

Chapter Three

Dad is driving me home from work, questioning me about homework and school in that half-automatic way parents sometimes do, when my phone buzzes inside my backpack. He stops in midsentence and looks at me. Dad thinks it's rude to talk on your cell phone or text when you're with a live person. I'm *supposed* to turn off my phone and check messages later, but what Dad doesn't get is that "later" is always too late for a text. The whole point is that it's instant. If I don't pick up right away, I'll get six more texts saying, "**where r u?**" or "**turn on yr PHONE!**"

"It's got to be Jess," I say. "Can't I just look?"

"You *can*," he says in that but-I'll-be-so-disappointed

tone. Do parents take classes in acting this way? When I grow up, I will *never* guilt-trip my kids about anything stupid. You heard it here first.

I decide to put up with Dad's sigh and flip open my phone. Jess's text says:

cool news fm 4-J!!!

"4-J" is our code name for Jason. It stands for "Fourth Jonas," because he has great curly hair and looks just a bit like Nick Jonas.

I have to ask. Using both thumbs, I type:

what???

Sure enough, just like clockwork, Dad sighs. But it's worth it for Jess's response:

he bought masq ball tix 4 me & him!

He *bought* two tickets, when Amelia could get us in free? It *is* for a good cause, and if I could afford it, I'd certainly want to make a donation, but still. What can I say but:

whoa!

Jess types back:

i know, right?

Dad clears his throat loudly. "Sorry," I say as my thumbs quickly type:

gotta go TTYS

I show Dad the phone and say, "I'm turning it off, see?"

"It's just not polite to the person you're with. It's like saying the text's more important than —"

"— being with someone," I say along with him. "Got it."

Dad grins. "Have I said that before a few times?"

"Um . . . maybe one or two. Hundred."

This makes him laugh very hard. One thing I love about Dad is that he has a sense of humor about himself. That's rare in grown-ups. And absolutely *extinct* in my stepmother.

Fay greets us with, "The salmon is getting dried out," which is not my idea of how to welcome your husband and stepdaughter home. Nice seeing you, too, Fay.

It's true, though. Her salmon tastes like fish-flavored cardboard, with some kind of mustard sauce smeared on the top. Ashley takes one bite and spits it into her napkin with a loud, "Yuck!" Brynna refuses to try hers at all. If I pulled that, Fay would be furious, but she just reaches over and gives the twins more mashed potatoes and peas, then asks if they'd rather have fish sticks.

Well, hello, who wouldn't? But I've got my eyes on a bigger prize — getting to go to the Hunger Unmasked Ball — so I swallow my salmon as if it were the tastiest thing ever. My Fay-wrangling skills are improving, and I know if I ask her directly, the answer is bound to be no. Anyway, I don't want to be grilled about how I'm going to pay for my ticket (not) or who's going to drive (Jess's mother, I hope) or who I'm going to go with (Jess, Jason, and . . . um).

That's a tough one. It *would* be really fun to bring Will, who loves anything having to do with live music, but do I have the nerve to invite him? Jess bringing 4-J makes the whole event feel . . . different. I mean, just *seeing* the word *couple* made me and Will blush and get stupid in front of our lockers.

Not for the first time, I envy Jess having a boyfriend who's already asked her out. And now Jason's buying their tickets, as if it was nothing for an eighth grader to plunk down a hundred and fifty bucks for a dance. They're acting like miniature grown-ups. It's *weird*.

29

I'm not ready to go there. And Will isn't either. That part is for sure.

As soon as I get the table cleared off and the dishwasher loaded, I head upstairs and log on to my laptop. Before I go into my messages, I stop to stare at my Adam Kessler wallpaper. His eyes are like twin swimming pools. What if he *did* come to Hunger Unmasked, and I got to dance with him again? I can feel my heart flutter and fizz at the thought. Then I go to the Web site for Hunger Unmasked.

There are photos from last fall's ball, and some of the masquerade costumes are gorgeous. I sure hope Amelia can make this work. I hate to think what would happen to her — or to me — if she got caught letting me in with no ticket.

I don't want to think about that any more than I have to, so I click on the link that says *Entertainment*. I wonder if maybe the poster was printed a while ago, and the Web site has more up-to-date information. Like *names*.

No such luck — it just says "Special guest stars from Broadway shows *Angel* and *Bye Bye Birdie!*" with photos of both shows' full casts. Adam's wearing his Western outlaw costume from Act Two, and he has an adorable smile on his face, like he still can't believe he's the star of a big Broadway musical. As if being so cute weren't enough, he's also a really nice guy. Not to mention a super-sensational actor and singer.

Stop me before I start swooning.

Two boring homework hours later, my phone rings.

"Can you believe this?" says Jess. Her voice is so bubbly I can practically see the grin that comes with it. "I just asked if he wanted to *go*, since Amelia sounds pretty sure she can sneak us in for free, but he said a lot of kids from the Foreman Academy are going and he'd buy my ticket." I notice that Jess doesn't even bother to use Jason's name anymore. She talks about him so much that there's only one possible "he."

"Well, I guess you're all taken care of," I say, trying not to sound left out.

"Hey, I bet Amelia can get you and Will in, no sweat. One couple's got to be simpler than two."

"Except we're not a couple."

"Oh, puh-leeze!" says Jess. "You two are ridiculous."

"Will *isn't* my boyfriend," I tell her. "He's just a friend."

"Who is totally into you, and you're totally into him, but okay, whatever. Just ask your *friend* Will if he wants to sneak into a masquerade ball with live music and Broadway stars, free. If you think he's going to say no, then you're totally hopeless and I'm hanging up on you."

Tough love, Jess Munson style. "Okay, fine."

"So you'll ask him? *Tomorrow.*"

"I'll ask him tomorrow," I say, and hang up, thinking, *Help*.

And of course the next day, I run right into Will at his locker. The door is wide open, and he's got a roll of Scotch tape in one hand. I have to ask. "What are you doing?"

"Oh," he says, looking embarrassed. He steps back to show me the inside of the door, where he's taped up some *Rolling Stone* magazine covers with photos of his favorite bands. "I liked how you put all your acting stuff up, so . . ."

My acting stuff? Leave it to Will not to notice the photos on my locker door are all of cute guys! But you know
what, they *are* all actors, so maybe he's kind of right.

"That is mad cool," I say, smiling a little too wide. Will
pushes back his bangs, which as usual fall right back over
his eyes. He has really nice eyebrows, but you'd never
know it.

"I like being reminded there's life outside school. You
know?" Will looks at me, and I nod. Why does my tongue
feel so thick in my mouth, as if I were eating a mitten? If
I try to talk, it'll come out all vowels. But I promised Jess,
and now Will's given me the perfect opening.

"Speaking of life outside school . . ." And my voice just
dries up. He's looking at me, waiting for me to finish. My
ears feel warm. There's no way I'm not going to blush as I
ask my *friend* Will to . . . to a *dance*. That is so much like
asking a guy on a date. It *is* asking a guy on a date. I can't
do this. Sorry, Jess.

"Diana wants to know if you'll join her and me and
some other cool peeps at that masquerade ball thing," says
Jess, very casual, suddenly standing behind us. I stare. Did
I channel her?

Will turns toward her. "The Hunger Unmasked thing? Doesn't it cost, like —"

"Amelia says she can get you in free. Ethan's going. And Jason, you know him, too. It'll be awesome." Jess sounds totally at ease and comfortable, as if she invites guys to events every day.

"Sure," Will says.

"Really?" I blurt, way too happy.

He nods. "Sounds like fun."

Now I *am* blushing. I can feel it spread up from my neck to my cheeks. "There's live music by . . . that band," I say idiotically, trying to fill the silence. Better let Jess do the talking.

"Do you have a suit you can wear?" she demands. "It's formal wear."

Will just says, "Not really." He looks at me, helpless.

"Well, what are you planning to go as for Halloween?" Jess asks. "Maybe that would work."

Will shifts from one foot to another. "I was thinking of, um . . . Kurt Cobain."

Jess hoots. "From Nirvana? That is so Will Carson! What would you *wear*?"

34

He shrugs. "Flannel shirt, grungy jeans?"

"Will, you wear that every day! How would anyone know it's a costume?" Jess turns toward me. "Will needs a makeover, pronto. I leave it in your helpful hands. Gotta go, I've got homeroom downstairs."

And she's gone just as suddenly as she appeared. Will and I look at each other, feeling even more awkward. I have to say *something*. "Flannel and grunge doesn't sound very masquerade ball. Maybe something a bit more dressed up?"

Will thinks. "My dad's got a really sharp tux from his drummer days. It's kind of vintage."

"That sounds totally perfect! And how about a mask?"

He shakes his head, then says, "Oh, wait! I've got one! It's a Mexican wrestler mask — it pulls over your head, it's bright yellow with red spiderwebs and a —"

I can't help it. I burst out laughing.

"No, huh?" Will sounds disappointed. "I love that thing."

"I can make you a mask," I tell him. And then I surprise myself. "I'm really glad you're coming."

Will turns bright red and mutters, "Me, too," as he buries his face in his locker. I hurry toward mine. That's *enough*.

35

Jess and I celebrate after school, and I tell her about Will's dad's tuxedo. "And what are *you* planning to wear?" I ask.

"Oh, right," says Jess, who has clearly not given it one second's thought. "How about that green dress I wore to the Foreman Academy dance?"

"It's supercute, but it's short. Isn't a ball gown supposed to be floor-length? Besides, Jason's seen it already."

"Oh, right. If you weren't such a stilt-walker, I'd borrow that gorgeous black-and-white dress Nelson sewed for you to wear to *Angel*." Jess is four inches shorter than me, which almost makes up for her having amazing red hair when mine's just plain brown. Almost. I don't remind her that the black-and-white dress was short, too, or that it got torn in the door of our limo. (Isn't that a great phrase to use in a sentence? "The door of *our limo*." It sounds even better with an English accent, like I had that night.)

But then I remember my offer from Nelson. "Hey!" I

say, "you should come to the cleaners." And I tell Jess how Nelson needs more hands this weekend, and offered me tailoring lessons in trade. She gets my point instantly.

"I am so there! Tell Nelson I'm on it!"

"I will," I say, giving Jess a quick hug and rushing onto my bus just before the door shuts.

Lara is working at the cash register for the third day in a row, which is weird. In the old days, Cat and Elise took turns, one at the customer counter and one bagging clothes in the back, but the old days are gone. When I go to pick up the first cartload of drop-off clothes, I greet Lara with a perfectly friendly hello and get a cold stare in return.

There's a hideous Halloween sweater-vest, with an appliqué black cat, sitting on the top of the cart. If Cat was up front, we'd be trading jokes about what first-grade teacher bought that at what mall. But with Joyless and Lara both giving me the evil eye, there's nothing to do but roll the bin into the workroom as fast as I can.

As I'm dumping the dirty clothes onto the sorting table, Cat hurries in, late as usual, snapping her smock. Her eye goes straight to the vest. "*Ay, Dios mio*, who did the artwork on that? That black cat's got a hairball for sure."

"And check out the candy-corn buttons." I point at them.

"Woof," says Cat, laughing. "That one goes into the Fashion Hall of Shame."

This is the way I like work to be. As long as you're getting the job done, why not have fun, too?

"Is it just me," I ask Cat as she helps me sort clothes, "or is Lara on some kind of power trip?"

"It is not just you, trust me," says Cat. "She used to be nice when she worked in the back, but now she's like Joyless's Mini-Me."

This makes me laugh really hard. I love Cat.

"Whoops," she says, picking up a suit jacket that's tagged for tailoring. "This goes to Nelson. You want to bring it?"

"My pleasure," I tell her, and head for the Tailoring section.

Just as I'd hoped, Nelson's delighted to hear Jess can join me this weekend. "I'm busy on Saturday," he says, "but I'll be here bright and early on Sunday A.M., hyped up on caffeine. Tell Redhead to bring something she'd like to alter. That green dress sounds fabulous."

Sunday is our family brunch day. But Dad's so tickled by the idea of me wanting to learn tailoring skills that he agrees to drop me and Jess off at the cleaners first thing in the morning, when he goes out to buy pastries. We stop at LaToria's Bakery first, and the mingled smells of freshly baked bread and chocolate chip cookies make us giddy. Jess and I stand in front of the pastry case, trying to figure out what to eat.

"No chocolate, no sticky buns, no powdered sugar," I tell her. "Nelson will freak."

Jess rolls her eyes. "I can wash my *hands*."

Just then the baker fills a bin with still-warm croissants, and the what-to-get argument's over. We eat them in the car on the way to Cinderella Cleaners, washing the treats down with containers of milk.

It feels funny to see the whole parking lot empty and no lights on inside customer service, just one in the Tailoring section.

"It looks so peaceful, doesn't it?" Dad says. He pulls right up to the front door, then gets out to unlock it with his heavy key ring as Jess and I climb out. She has her green dress inside a shopping bag so Dad won't see it. The fewer questions we have to answer, the better.

"Thanks for the ride," I say, stretching up to give Dad a kiss.

"And for breakfast," says Jess. "Best croissants *ever*."

"Have fun with Nelson," Dad says. "You're going to learn from the master." He gets back in the car, giving two toots on the horn as he backs away.

"Come on," I say, leading Jess to the Tailoring section. I can hear music spilling out from behind the closed door, not the soft background Muzak Loretta and Sadie prefer, but something that sounds hip and catchy, with African drums.

"What *is* that song?" asks Jess as I open the door.

Nelson looks up from the cutting table, where he's piecing together a colorful patchwork of diamond-shaped pieces. "That is my main man K'naan," he announces. "And you two are covered with crumbs. Outside." He gestures us back through the door.

"Whoa," whispers Jess as we brush our coats into the wastebasket. "You weren't kidding!" We come back in, spotless, and Nelson smiles.

"That's what I'm talking about," he says.

"What are you making?" I ask him. "Is that for the ball?"

"Afraid so," he says. "It's a family who ordered traditional Venetian Carnivale costumes. The wife and daughter are easy — your basic red-and-gold shepherdess gowns — and the boy's is a red-and-gold clown suit, but Dad wants a Harlequin cape. Mucho labor-intensive."

"How can we help?" I ask.

"You get the fun part. Hats and masks."

"Coolness!" breathes Jess, her eyes wide.

Nelson sets us up at a worktable with bins full of glitter trim, sequins, and feathers. "You know how to use a hot glue gun, right? Here are my sketches." He opens a folder. Inside are the most stunning drawings I've ever seen. The gowns are a total fantasy, with glittering masks and feather-topped headdresses shaped like the sun and the moon. The two-tone clown suit is topped off with a jester's hat, and the Harlequin has a tricorner that looks like George Washington crossing Las Vegas.

41

I'm in awe. "Nelson, these are *outrageous*!"

"Of course they are," he says briskly, dumping a bag of blank masks on the table. "Here are the forms. Follow my sketch, but have fun with the details. Basically, you can't go over the top. It's like Mardi Gras — it's all about *more*."

"Why are there six?" Jess asks, and I realize there are two extra mask forms.

"Oh," Nelson says with a smile. "Just in case you mess up. If you don't, then the extras are yours to decorate. Call it a tip."

"That's mega cool!" Jess exclaims, and I'm with her 100 percent.

"Oh, and I picked up one more for someone Diana just might have invited," says Nelson, digging his hand deeper into the bag. "You know, that boy you swear isn't your boyfriend."

"He *isn't*!" I say as Jess cracks up laughing. Nelson pulls out a black half-mask form, the kind that just covers the top of your face. It's perfect, but . . . "How did you know that?" I demand. Nelson met Will when he was working on the Tasha Kane video with Will's father, but that doesn't answer my question.

"Very mysterious," Nelson says, tapping his forehead. "You told me."

That's right, I did, when I asked him if Jess could come, and we talked about what all my friends would be wearing for their masquerade costumes. Now I feel really dumb. "Well, he's still not my boyfriend."

"Whatever you say," Nelson says. "Here's his mask."

Jess and I spend the next few hours happily hot-gluing sequins and jewels onto the Carnivale masks and attaching feathers and trim to the hats while Nelson speed-sews the costumes. He's pretty hands-off, but from time to time he checks in with suggestions, or calls us over to demonstrate sewing techniques.

"This is a dart," he says, showing us a solid triangle with a dotted line on his pattern. It looks like the nose of a paper airplane. "You're going to be using these to take in that pink gown. Here, put a straight pin through there, so the sides come together."

"Like this?" I start to put it in on a diagonal.

"Parallel to the fold. Easier to take out as you're running it through the machine. Okay, now two more pins. Top, middle, point. Got it?"

I nod, eagerly soaking up every last detail. When it's "not make or break," Nelson lets me and Jess use the sewing machines on things like interior seams so we get some practice.

The most nerve-racking part is using the pinking shears on fabric that somebody's paid for. "Relax, it's the back of the painting," Nelson says, but I can't slice my shears through the shimmery satin without holding my breath. He asks me and Jess several times whether we need a break, but we're having much too much fun to be hungry.

It's almost two o'clock when Nelson sews the last ruffle onto the neck of the clown suit. "Lunch," he declares, standing up from his sewing machine. "With or without you, I'm going to Sam's Diner. I'm in dire need of a cheeseburger, medium rare."

The word *cheeseburger* jump-starts my appetite. I'm suddenly starving. Jess and I unplug our glue guns, and all three of us head for the diner next door.

"Booth in the window for me and the Dream Team," Nelson tells Tessie the hostess, who smiles at him like he's a regular.

"Hiya, Diana," she says in her New Jersey drawl, which makes my name sound like *Doyanna*. "How's ya Dad? Such a sweet man."

"He's good," I say, and we order three cheeseburgers, medium rare. While we're eating, Nelson fills us in on his whirlwind life, working in Tasha Kane's costume shop and now shuttling between part-time jobs at Cinderella Cleaners and a new TV series with Tasha's designer.

Jess's eyes are wide. "Wow," she says.

"Nelson's also going to try out for the next season of *Project Runway*," I say.

"You totally should," Jess says, swirling her last french fry through ketchup. "You would be *perfect*."

"That's what I keep telling them," Nelson says. "Sooner or later they'll wake up and smell the espresso. But for now, it's you guys' turn on the Hunger Unmasked Challenge. Let's make it work. You ready to roll?"

We nod eagerly. "Good," he says. "Go wash your hands."

Back at the cleaners, Jess pulls her green dress from the shopping bag and holds it in front of her body. Nelson studies it, arms folded across his chest. "I'm getting Mermaid Parade vibes," he says. "In a good way."

"We still have some green and blue sequins," says Jess, looking at the Carnivale hats and masks we've completed. I have to admit, they look fabulous. So do the costumes that Nelson has hung on four hangers along the back wall.

"Let's look at No Pickup and see if there's a good base for the dress's new bottom," Nelson suggests. "If not, we can patchwork my remnants bin."

We go into the workroom, which as always looks eerie with all the machines sitting silent. Nelson snaps on the lights, and we pass under the high row of plastic-bagged garments. At the No Pickup rack, I zero in on a shimmery silver-blue tablecloth. "How's this?" I say, peeling the tagged plastic bag off and handing the fabric to Nelson.

"Bingo!" he exclaims, pulling it off its wide hanger.

"This has mermaid tail written all over it. Good eye, Diana. Now let's see *your* look."

I hold up the pink dress and Jess gasps out loud. "OMG, that is the *ultimate*!" she says. "You are so lucky to work here!"

Right at the moment, I'd have to agree.

Chapter Four

After our great Sunday afternoon, Monday morning comes as a very rude shock. In all the excitement about getting to work on our gowns and masks for the ball, I somehow forgot I was facing my personal nightmare: a French test.

My French teacher, Madame Lefkowitz, looks and sounds like an owl. She wears big black-framed glasses and hunches her head so far down and forward that it looks as if it's growing out of her shoulders, with no neck at all. Her voice is raspy and hoarse, and even when she's speaking French, she has a New Jersey accent as thick as the Sam's Diner hostess's.

"Bone-JURE, class," she greets us, and we echo, "Bonjour, Madame Lefkowitz."

Then she tells us to take out our number two pencils, and my heart stops beating. It's *only* the end-of-the-quarter review test, worth 30 percent of our grade! How could I have forgotten?

For about the millionth time, I curse myself for taking French when all my friends signed up for Spanish. My mother spoke French, and she and Dad went to Paris for their honeymoon, and she always told me she wanted to take me to her favorite city. That can't ever happen, of course, but every time I think about transferring to Spanish, I remember Mom dipping a croissant into her coffee and telling me in a breathless, happy voice how the sidewalk cafés in France serve hot cocoa in big steaming bowls and how I'm going to love it.

Maybe I'll get there someday. But meanwhile, what do I do about this football-size knot in my stomach? I hate taking tests when I *am* prepared, and without any friends to remind me, I just plain forgot about doing the unit review. As Madame Lefkowitz passes out test sheets, I rack my brain, trying to think about what we've just covered. Irregular verbs, compound numbers, and parts of the body.

I wonder how you say "I am so dead!" in French.

• • •

The test is awful. I'm so nervous I can't even remember the things I *do* know, and some of these words, I swear, I've never seen in my life. It doesn't help my mood to find out from my friends at lunch that the fun Spanish teacher, Señorita Vásquez, is planning a classroom party to celebrate the Mexican Day of the Dead, which is right after Halloween. They're going to decorate skeleton figurines, eat traditional Mexican foods, and perform songs and skits. I'm totally jealous.

The only good news is that Kayleigh is back at her usual table, with her usual sidekick, Savannah, and the other popular girls. Ethan is sitting with them, but he doesn't look happy. Will's in the band room, practicing on his euphonium. (His main instrument is electric bass, but they don't have one of those in the Weehawken Middle School Marching Band.) So it's just our BFF foursome today.

Jess is describing her mermaid costume and the super-cool masks we made — hers is silver with seashells and pearls, mine has black sequins that echo the dress and lace trim. I kept Will's pretty simple so he won't be embarrassed. It's plain black with black-and-white checkered trim around the outside edge and the eyeholes.

"Speaking of costumes," says Sara, "we still haven't settled our Halloween plans." Sara has to work at her family's restaurant on Friday nights, so she's sick of hearing us go on and on about Hunger Unmasked.

"Zombie lunch ladies," says Jess automatically. "Day-Glo hairnets and aprons."

"I thought we were doing punk fairies," Amelia says.

"Fairies are a yawn," says Jess. "Total third grade."

"Not if they're *punk* fairies," Sara says. "We can spike up our hair, wear cool jewelry, put safety pins through our black wings."

That actually sounds kind of fun — I've got some great eighties accessories, and I could recycle the Pretty in Pink gown — but I'm loyal to Jess. "Zombie lunch ladies is more original," I declare.

"Score!" says Jess. "Zombie lunch ladies rule!"

"How do you figure that?" asks Amelia. "I'm counting two and two. We need a tiebreaker."

Jess turns around in her chair and calls, "Yo, Ethan! Get over here!"

Kayleigh's eyes narrow as Ethan stands and heads straight for our table. "What's up?" he says. "Got to be better than hearing what Savannah and Kayleigh just bought at the mall."

"Hey," Jess says, "you're the one dating her."

"Eat your heart out," grins Ethan.

"Puh-leeze! In your dreams," Jess shudders. They've been teasing each other like this for years. Ethan opens his mouth to reply, but Sara is faster.

"What should the four of us go as for Halloween, punk fairies or zombie lunch ladies?" she asks him.

"Which one did Munson pick? I vote the opposite."

"Not fair!" Jess exclaims. "We need a neutral vote."

"Hey, you called me over," grins Ethan.

"Here," says Amelia, always practical. She digs in her purse and passes out four index cards. "Everyone write down your favorite and fold it in quarters. We'll put them all in a bag and Ethan can pick one. Okay?"

We all nod and write down our suggestions. Ethan tries to look over Jess's shoulder and she covers her index card with her hand. One by one, we fold up our note cards and put them into Sara's empty lunch bag. As Amelia shakes them up, holding the bag out to Ethan, Jess says, "Wait!"

52

and points at the door, where Will's just come in with an armload of sheet music. "Neutral vote."

I get the same breathless catch in my throat I always feel when I see Will these days.

Ethan is protesting, "That's nuts! I'm so neutral it's *sick*!"

"I nominate Will," says Jess, and Sara, who's friends with him, too, says quickly, "I second!"

"I third," says Amelia.

Well, what can I say but "I fourth"?

Will lopes over to join us. He's wearing black jeans and a faded red T-shirt with a vintage photo of The Doors. "What's up?" he asks.

"We're stuck between zombies and fairies. Put your hand in this bag and pick a card," Jess says, and he does.

"That better not be Jess Munson's," says Ethan as Will unfolds it and reads out loud, "Vampire Prom Queens."

"WHAT?" says Jess. "Let me see that." She grabs the card out of Will's hands. There it is, in black and white. Sara's jaw drops and I do a double take.

Amelia just shrugs. "I changed my vote."

"You can't do that!" Jess snorts.

"I just said to write down your favorite," Amelia answers calmly. "Not that it had to be one or the other."

"Actually, I kind of love the idea of Vampire Prom Queens," I say, feeling suddenly excited. "And we've already got masquerade gowns. Just add some fake fangs and we're good to go."

"You three have masquerade gowns," Sara pouts. "I'll be busing tables at Masala."

"How about your sari?" I ask. "With fangs and a little tiara . . ."

"We could get red contact lenses, like Dakota Fanning in *New Moon*," Jess suggests, getting into it.

"Ew!" Sara says. "Way too creepy." But she's grinning, and we all agree that our Halloween costumes will rock.

Even Ethan and Will.

Right after school, Jess and I make a beeline to Ms. Wyant's classroom. I haven't been able to go to a Drama Club meeting since I started work at the cleaners, so it feels very nostalgic to see all the curtain-call photos and posters from shows on the wall. Ms. Wyant's erasing the blackboard from her last class, but as soon as she sees us, she puts down the eraser and starts to applaud. "Standing ovation," she says. "How's it going, Diana? We miss you at Drama Club!"

"I miss you, too," I say.

"Is the prop closet open for Halloween borrows?" asks Jess, always one to get right to the point.

"If you sign items out and agree to replace anything that gets damaged, I don't see why not," says Ms. Wyant. "What are you looking for?"

"Crowns and tiaras," says Jess.

"And the elbow-length gloves I wore in *My Fair Lady*," I add eagerly. "Those were so elegant."

"Help yourselves," says Ms. Wyant, and she opens the closet, with its shelves full of derby hats, papier-mâché goblets, foam swords, costume jewelry, and a vintage dial phone. It's like seeing a history of every show I've been in, and I realize all over again how much I miss acting. I guess I'll just have to make do with the putting-on-costumes part for now.

Jess has already bagged two gold plastic crowns and a rhinestone tiara. "These are awesome!" she says. "I'll sign out for these and the gloves, okay, Diana? You better get going or you'll miss your bus."

I nod breathlessly. "Thank you, Ms. Wyant!" I call as I rush for the door.

I leave school feeling great. Four more days till the coolest weekend of my whole life: the Hunger Unmasked Ball on Friday, and trick-or-treating with my best friends on Saturday. What can go wrong?

That's never a very smart question to ask when you live with my stepmother. Later that night, as I'm clearing away dinner dishes, I realize that I still need Fay's permission to go out this Friday night. Not only that, but I absolutely don't want her to know where I'm going. I don't like to tell outright lies, but it wouldn't be stretching the truth to say that I've made plans with Jess. I don't have to mention the detail about Amelia sneaking us into a fancy masquerade ball. Right?

Luckily, tonight's dinner is good — it's hard to mess

up three-cheese tortellini — so I can butter Fay up without lying at all.

"That was terrific," I tell her as I bring the plates to the kitchen, adding, "Ashley and Brynna had seconds."

Fay frowns. "They'd eat carbs and cheese every day if I let them."

"I ate broccoli, too!" Brynna calls from the dining room.

"What do you want, a gold medal?" grumps Ashley, who can't stand green vegetables.

"Ashley's picking on me!" Brynna yelps.

"Cut it out, girls," Fay snaps at them.

So much for buttering her up.

I bide my time, wrapping up leftovers, loading the dishwasher, and scrubbing the pots while Dad reads the paper at the kitchen table and Fay goes to change into more casual clothes. When she comes back to the kitchen, her hair's still sprayed into its frosted-blond helmet, and her gold earrings and office makeup look weird with a pink velour tracksuit. But maybe she feels more relaxed now. I try again.

"Can I go over to Jess's on Friday night?" I ask. I've already figured out my cover story — we're planning to work on our Halloween costumes (again, not that far from the truth) — but I don't get a chance to explain my plans.

"Your father and I are going out," Fay says brusquely. "I need you to stay with the twins."

"Again?" Brynna whines from the dining room, where she and Ashley are now playing Guess Who. "You go out *all the time*."

"That's enough out of you, young lady," says Fay. "We barely ever go out."

Only when I want to do something else.

Dad looks up from the paper. "If Diana's got plans, I can stay with the girls."

Fay slams a cabinet closed. "You cannot keep doing this, Frank! These are people I work with. It isn't an *option*. We're going together and that is that."

"All right, all right," Dad says hastily. "I just thought I could join your coworkers for dinner, but not for this party thing afterward. That way Diana could —"

"You're *always* taking her side!" Fay says angrily.

58

Maybe because you do the opposite, I want to tell her, but I bite my tongue, since whatever I say will be wrong.

"I'm not taking her side. I'm trying to offer a compromise," Dad says.

"Some compromise! She gets what she wants, and you get what you want. Well, what about *me*? I am so tired of begging and pushing you, every step of the way." Her voice is getting shriller, and Dad looks so unhappy I feel really guilty.

"I don't like big social events, Fay. You know that," he says, doing his best to sound reasonable. "I just want to see if there's any way we could manage —" The phone cuts him off in midsentence. Fay grabs it.

"Hello?" she says, her voice going suddenly sugary. "Oh. How are you, Alison?" She listens a moment, then says, "For Marissa's birthday?"

Ashley and Brynna sit up like a couple of prairie dogs, ears perked and waiting for news. Marissa is one of their closest friends.

"Yes, I'm sure they would love it. When?" Fay's face creases into a frown. "*This* Friday? I'll have to see, we've got plans and . . ."

"Mo-om!" both twins yell in unison. Sometimes they really are spooky.

"Let me get back to you. Thanks." Fay hangs up, glaring at the twins. "Be *quiet* when I'm on the phone. I get business calls on this number."

"That was Marissa's mom," Ashley says in a know-it-all voice, and Brynna pipes in, "What's this Friday?"

Fay takes a deep breath. "Marissa is having a sleepover party."

"On Friday? That's perfect!" says Dad. "That solves everything. The twins get to go to Marissa's, Diana is free for the evening, and I . . ." He gets up, slipping his arms around Fay. "I get to take my sweet wife where she wants to go."

"Don't be sarcastic," says Fay, and I feel like screaming at her. Dad just gave up what he wanted, *and* gave her a hug, and that isn't enough for her?

What ever would be enough? I wonder. I promised Dad I'd be nicer to Fay, and I'm doing my best, even though it feels like a mask I put on every day. But she's really not making it easy.

Chapter Five

The good news, of course, is that now I can go to the masquerade ball without any obstacles. Except for the having-no-tickets part.

What if Amelia gets caught sneaking me and Will into the ball? I wonder the next day. I've stuck my own neck out plenty of times when there was something I really wanted to do. But now it feels like I'm sticking somebody else's neck out even farther than mine.

"Are you sure you're okay with this?" I ask Amelia as we're getting ready for gym class. "I don't want to get you in trouble."

"You're kidding me, right?" she says. "This has changed my attitude about having to work at this thing by, like, a hundred and eighty degrees. It'll be great to have all you guys there, for starters. And I love a challenge."

This is true. Amelia is always happiest when she has something to work out and win, whether it's soccer strategy or a tough math problem. She even loves taking tests, which I totally can't understand. Sara, who's good at more or less everything, likes to joke that Amelia and I each have one half of the perfect school brain. In an ideal world, Amelia could take all my math classes, sports, and tests for me, and I could ace all the creative stuff that she thinks she can't handle.

"Okay, if you're sure," I reply. "And I owe you a favor."

"Don't sweat it," Amelia says, grinning from ear to ear as we enter the gym. She looks the way I do when I go onstage.

Jess is at least as excited as I am about getting to go to the Hunger Unmasked Ball. She and 4-J have been texting nonstop about costumes, and getting permission from parents, and who else is going to come from the Foreman Academy.

Then I get a surprise on Thursday morning, when Will comes up to me at my locker and tells me he tried on his father's vintage tuxedo last night.

"Did it fit?" I ask. I'm psyched that he's getting into this.

"Sort of." Will shifts from one foot to the other, embarrassed. "The pants are too big. And the jacket's got mad giant shoulders."

I laugh. "Shoulder pads? That is so eighties!"

"I guess. I'm pretty glad I'll be wearing a mask," Will says.

"You'll love it," I promise, and head off to homeroom with a really big smile on my face.

That smile stays in place until French class. Madame Lefkowitz's door is plastered with posters of the Eiffel Tower, berets, and a lumpy French actor named Gérard Depardieu. As soon as I walk through it, I can tell something's wrong. Madame Lefkowitz looks at me, hunches her head farther back on her shoulders, and sniffs, *"Qu'est-ce qui est arri-VAY?,"* which means, "What happened?" Before I can answer, the bell rings, and everyone takes their seats.

Madame Lefkowitz doesn't waste any time. As soon as we've finished our ritual greeting of "Bone-JURE, class" and "Bonjour, Madame," she starts passing back tests, sometimes adding a comment like *"C'est très BONE, Rebecca."* My palms start to sweat. When she gets to my desk, she pauses, then hands me a paper with the lowest grade I've ever gotten. My stomach caves in as if somebody punched me.

"See me after class," Madame Lefkowitz says, as if I wouldn't understand her if she spoke in French. And she's probably right.

I'm so upset about my terrible grade that I can't concentrate for the rest of the class. Which means that I won't have a clue how to do tonight's homework, and I'll do even worse on the next test, and probably flunk French altogether, and not graduate middle school, and wind up as a hobo. All because I forgot to study last weekend.

It's not easy being dramatic.

At long last the bell rings, and I drag myself up to Madame Lefkowitz's desk. "This won't do, Doy-yanna," she says.

"I'm so sorry," I tell her. "Can I retake it?"

"That wouldn't be feh," she says, and it takes me a moment to realize that she means *fair*. "But if you want extra credit, you could make a travel bro-SHAW."

"A brochure?" I ask.

She nods. "For a French-speaking country, with the text in French. Bring it in Monday. And I'll need ya parents to sign that test."

My heart lurches inside my chest. "You mean both of them?"

Madame Lefkowitz looks me right in the eye and says, *"Oui."*

Getting Dad and Fay to sign that test would be bad enough, but that isn't the end of my troubles. As I'm crossing the parking lot toward the cleaners, I see Lara watching me through the plate glass front window, her eyes narrowed into two slits. I wonder why she's got it in for me. Is it just because I'm the owner's daughter? When I first started working at Cinderella Cleaners, some people seemed to hold that against me, but everyone's nice to me now.

Except MacInerny, but she doesn't know how to spell the word *nice*.

I go in through the back, grab my smock, and go to the locker room to stash my backpack. One of my Converse high-tops is loose, so I bend down to retie my green and pink laces. When I straighten up, Lara is standing in front of me.

"I know vat you took," she says, folding her arms.

It might be her Russian accent, but at first I don't know what she's talking about. "What I took?"

"From No Pickup," says Lara, her fox-like eyes glinting. "I know about this."

If my heart stops one more time today, they'll be taking me to the emergency room. I don't know what to tell her. I can't pretend I didn't do it, and asking "Why do you care?" sounds like picking a fight.

When in doubt, say something bland.

"Oh," I say.

Lara just looks at me. "Where is this pink dress and this tablecloth? You must to return them."

"I can't," I say, wincing. "I used them to make Halloween costumes."

Lara raises her eyebrows. I can't help feeling that she's enjoying this more than she should. "Customer who owns tablecloth came in for late pickup this morning," she says. "How vill your father explain that it's now Halloveen costume?"

All right, call the paramedics and carry me out on a stretcher. My poor heart is stopping for good.

How could Nelson and I have forgotten to look at the date on the tag before we turned that tablecloth into a mermaid tail? Garments are supposed to be kept in No Pickup for thirty days before they get claimed by employees or given to charity. I did check the tag on the prom dress way back when I first found it, so I knew it was ready to claim. But the tablecloth wasn't, apparently. The last thing I want to do is get Nelson in trouble after all he did for me and Jess, so I'll take the blame for not checking the date on its tag.

"I don't know," I say, doing my best not to burst into tears. "I guess I'll have to pay the customer for a replacement. Does my father know about this?"

"He knows it is missink," says Lara. "I know that you took it. I have seen you at No Pickup rack many times. Shall I tell this to your father?"

67

She's staring at me in that same icy, satisfied way, and I get the weird feeling she's trying to bribe me. I won't tell your father if . . . what? What could I possibly have that would satisfy Lara Nekrasova? Maybe she just likes to play with her prey, like a cat with a mouse.

"I better tell him myself," I say. "He's my boss, too."

Lara raises her eyebrows again. "As you vish."

As I *wish*? I *wish* that I'd looked at the tag and had not cut up that tablecloth. I *wish* I'd remembered to study for French. I *wish* I could hit rewind and replay the whole weekend. But this is real life, not a fairy tale. Nobody's granting me wishes.

I take a deep breath and walk into the workroom, so upset that I practically don't even notice the surge of machine noise and dry-cleaning smells. Lara follows me like a prison guard. What does she think, I'm going to bolt and hide out in Sam's Diner?

Cat started working before me today, and she's stretching up onto her tiptoes to hang some bagged clothes on the overhead conveyor belt. "Hey, Diana," she calls as I pass by. "I got a job here for a tall person."

"Can't talk now," I tell her. She takes one look at my face, sees Lara walking behind me, and says, "Uh-oh."

Exactly.

Dad's office door is ajar, and as I raise my hand to knock, the back of my throat feels so dry I can't swallow. "Come in," he calls out in his usual cheerful voice.

"Diana has somethink to tell you," says Lara. I have the awful sense she's going to follow me into Dad's office, but she turns and goes back to her place at the counter with her mentor and role model, Joyless. I close the door tight. I'm not going to give either one of them the satisfaction of listening in on this conversation.

"Hi, honey!" Dad says, getting up from his desk, which is covered with piles of receipts. He's so happy to see me that I want to sink through the floor. And of course, because Dad knows me better than anyone else on the planet, he notices it right away. "What's the matter?" he asks.

I grit my teeth and get right to the point. "You know that blue tablecloth from the No Pickup rack?"

"Did you take it, Diana?" Dad's voice is measured and calm, as it always is when he's upset with me. It's his I'm-disappointed-in-your-choices tone, and it's ten times worse than Fay's yelling.

I nod. "I'm so sorry."

"The customer came in to claim it this morning, and nobody knew where it was. It was very embarrassing. You need to give it right back to me."

"I can't," I say, wincing. "It's at Jess's."

Dad looks even more disappointed in me, but he keeps his voice even. "Then let's go and get it. I'll drive you to her house."

I shake my head miserably. "It isn't a tablecloth anymore. It's part of her Halloween costume."

"What?" That's his first flash of anger. I gulp.

"You know how we were working with Nelson on Sunday?"

Dad nods. "He showed me those red-and-gold Carnivale costumes this morning. But what's that got to do with —"

"I'm trying to tell you," I say, realizing I just interrupted him.

70

"I think you better," says Dad, and he sits on the edge of his desk with his arms folded over his chest.

I tell him the whole story: how Jess and I spent Sunday morning working for Nelson, and then he helped us sew our Halloween costumes. "Kind of like a trade," I say, talking too fast. "Jess's dress was too short, and we needed more fabric, and I took her to the No Pickup rack, and I spotted that tablecloth, just the right color. I thought it had been there the full thirty days and was up for grabs."

"But you didn't look at the date on the tag? You know that's the procedure."

"I guess I forgot," I say sheepishly. "I just pulled it out of the bag."

"And you . . . cut up a customer's property?"

I squirm, nodding my head.

"I can't hear you."

"Yes," I whisper. "I am so sorry."

Dad gets up and circles around to his desk chair. Without saying a word, he leans back and just looks at me. The silence is terrible.

"What's going to happen?" I ask in a cracked voice.

"I'm going to call up the customer and tell her that her tablecloth's been mislaid — I think that's more tactful than 'cut up for a Halloween costume,' don't you? — and I'll offer her full compensation."

"I can pay for it," I tell him quickly. "I earned all that money from being in Tasha Kane's video."

"Yes, I know that," says Dad. "And you already owe me quite a bit of it, if you remember."

Of course I remember. Dad just about lost one of his biggest clients, Lydia Felter, because I borrowed her daughter's cool vest when I went to Tasha Kane's soundstage. Dad calmed Mrs. Felter down with a gift certificate, which I'm going to pay for. I'm guessing he'll do the same thing for this tablecloth lady.

"You can't keep on buying your way out of trouble, Diana. And you've never gotten into this kind of trouble before." Dad looks at me. "Maybe you're just not grown-up enough to be working here."

My stomach drops. "Dad!" I protest. I can't believe it. Is he going to *fire* me?

"I'm still talking, Diana. Don't speak till I'm done." I nod, my heart pounding as he keeps his eyes fixed on mine.

"Now, I've cut you a whole lot of slack this fall. Time and again. And I don't like the decisions you've made. I thought having this job would be good for your character, but maybe it was a miscalculation."

Is he finished? I don't want to interrupt him again, but I have to say something.

"Dad, I'll do anything. If you don't want me to pay for it, think of some other punishment and I'll do it. But I love working here."

"You do?" says Dad. "Really and truly?"

"Of course I do. Yes."

Dad puts his hands on the desk. "You know who I think of whenever I sit here? Your grandpapa. When we spoke on the phone on Sunday, I told him that you were at the cleaners, learning how to do tailoring. He was so proud of you. So was I."

I'm too ashamed to speak. I look down at my toes as Dad goes on. "I just hope that tablecloth wasn't a gift from this poor woman's mother or grandmother. There are some things that can't be replaced."

"I know," I whisper. I can feel the tears stinging behind my eyes.

Dad notices right away. He says, "I think my point has been made. You will need to pay for this. And I'm suspending your right to take clothes from the No Pickup rack."

I gulp. That's been one of my favorite things about working at the cleaners — it's like having a free secondhand store. But I don't protest. I just hang my head and nod.

"I need to get back to work now, Diana. And so do you," Dad says. "Leave the door open for me, okay?"

"I will," I say, putting my hand on the doorknob. I can't stand it when Dad is upset with me.

"Anything else?" he says gently. I shake my head, pushing the door open. How am I going to find the courage to show him that French test?

It also takes courage to walk past the customer counter, where Joyless and Lara are watching me like a couple of crows at a roadkill. I don't make eye contact with either of them. I just keep my head down and go right to the bin full of clothes to be sorted, always my first task. As I'm rolling it toward the big double doors that go into the workroom, Nelson comes out from Tailoring.

"There you are!" he says to me, and to Joyless, "I need to borrow Diana for a minute. I'll bring her right back."

He grabs me by the elbow before MacInerny can say a word, leading me back to the Tailoring section. As soon as we're out of earshot, he hisses, "I'm so sorry about the tablecloth. I should have made sure that you'd checked the claim date. Did Lara get you into trouble?"

I don't want Nelson to feel any worse, so I just shrug and tell him, "No biggie."

He nods. "Come inside for a minute. There's someone I want you to meet."

Nelson opens the door to the Tailoring section. Inside is a country club–looking couple, about Dad's age, dressed up in two of the Carnivale costumes. They're holding their masks in their hands, and the woman looks vaguely familiar. She must be a regular customer.

"Did you help to make these?" she asks, raising her glittering sun mask in front of her face. "They're *adorable*!"

"She did more than help," Nelson says. "Diana *designed* those masks."

"Diana?" The dressing room curtain parts, and out comes a blond girl in another red-and-gold Carnivale ball gown, wearing my moon mask. It can't be. "*You* made my mask?" asks a voice I'd know anywhere and wish I didn't.

It's Kayleigh Carell.

Kayleigh takes off the moon mask, shaking out her blond hair. "That is just so outrageous!"

That's one way to put it. I glance at the fourth costume, still on its hanger. Unless Kayleigh has a brother that I've never heard of, that red-and-gold clown suit — the one for "the boy" — must be Ethan's.

Wait till Jess finds out that she made Ethan's mask!

"Are you two girls classmates?" bubbles Kayleigh's mother. "How charming. Were you in *Our Town*?" she asks me.

"Diana was working here so she couldn't try out," says Kayleigh in a phony too-bad, so-sad voice. "She is *such* a good actress."

"Oh, yes, you were in *My Fair Lady* last year," says her mother. "Adorable."

Kayleigh looks annoyed by this praise, but then she glances at her reflection in the three-way mirror. She gives a quick twirl so her full skirt swirls out like a red-and-gold

76

flower. "These gowns are fantastic," she says. "Too bad you won't get to see the ball, Diana."

Nelson raises his eyebrows. He knows perfectly well that I'm planning to go, so I send him an eye signal: *Don't say a word.* Being Nelson, he gets it.

"I have to get back to work," I tell Kayleigh, doing my best not to grit my teeth. "See you in school."

"Buh-bye," Kayleigh says with a syrupy smile.

Nelson opens the door for me, then follows me out. "I'm sorry," he whispers. "Again. I had no idea you knew her."

"You met her once before. Kayleigh came in with her mom when I first started working here."

"Really?" He shrugs. "Who remembers? Your basic Blake Lively wannabe, dime-a-dozen mean blonde."

Now *that* is a perfect description of Kayleigh Carell. I can't wait to step on her toes at the masquerade ball!

Dad's very quiet on the drive home from the cleaners. I wonder if he reached the customer who owned the blue tablecloth. I glance over at him several times, but I don't dare to ask what she said. I think about begging him not

77

to tell Fay, but I can't find the words for that either. Besides, I already know what he'd say: that he doesn't keep secrets from her.

What Dad doesn't realize is that this forces me to keep secrets from *him*. Like the masquerade ball. In the old days, Mom would have been thrilled at the thought of me getting to go to such an event. She would have helped me dress up, lent me jewelry, shared the whole fantasy with me. But I'm so certain that Fay will say no that I can't even tell her about it. Or Dad. Especially now that I'm in so much trouble.

Maybe I should just stay home. I can't stand the thought of missing out on the ball, but if I got caught sneaking in, after *this*, I might lose my job at the cleaners. I would hate that so much.

Plus I still need to get both their signatures on my French test. Like everything else, it's a question of finding the right time to ask.

I guess I could put it off till tomorrow morning, right before I'm leaving for school, but it wouldn't be wise. Dad and Fay would both know I was trying to dodge an in-depth conversation. And they would be right.

I sort through my options. Dinnertime is out. I don't want to be a bad role model for the twins, which I know is the way Fay would spin it. And bedtime is never the right time for anything.

Right after dinner looks like my best bet, I decide as Dad and I hang our coats in the hall closet. After I've been a good girl and cleaned up the kitchen, before I go upstairs to work on my homework, including that French-language travel brochure I'm doing to get extra credit.

So that's what I do. I wait till the twins are upstairs, watching *Hannah Montana* reruns for the ninetieth time. Dad is reading a mystery novel, and Fay's going over a house listing site on her laptop and jotting down notes. I pick up my school backpack and tell them that I have a French test I need them to sign.

Dad frowns. "You need us to sign it?"

"My grade's not very good," I say. "I'm really sorry." And I take the test out of my backpack.

Dad sucks in his breath as he looks at the paper. "Not very good is right. What was the problem?"

"You know how I am about tests. I get totally nervous, I make dumb mistakes."

"Did you study?" He's looking at me like he already knows that I didn't, and just wonders whether I'll tell him the truth. I better.

"I . . . Well, I . . . kind of forgot."

"You forgot," says Dad in the same I'm-disappointed tone he used in his office.

"Let me see this," says Fay, getting up from the table.

I wince. Here it comes. She looks at the paper and looks back at me. "This is disgraceful, Diana."

"I know," I say, looking at Dad for help. He doesn't say a word.

"You are grounded this weekend," Fay says.

"What?" I blurt out. "You can't ground me for not doing well on a test! I've got plans with Jess Friday night, and Saturday is Halloween! That's completely not fair!"

"You can't bring home grades like this," Fay says. "You're in eighth grade. This goes right on your transcript. Your permanent record."

"But I'm doing a project to get extra credit. Madame Lefkowitz says I can —"

"Fine. You can work on it this weekend."

"I've got the whole day wide open on Sunday!" My

80

voice rises, desperate. "You can't make me stay home on Halloween weekend!"

I look over at Dad, my eyes pleading. He won't let her be this harsh with me, will he? I know he's still mad about me cutting that customer's tablecloth, but —

"I agree with Fay," Dad says, and I feel like I've been slapped. "I'm not pleased with the way you've been acting, Diana."

"Thank you," says Fay to Dad. "Nice to get some support for once." She turns back to me. "Why are you even taking that French class? You should just take Spanish like everyone else. It's much easier. And Spanish is more useful anyway. Half of the people who work for your father are Mexican."

I take a deep breath. I can feel myself shaking with anger, but I keep my voice calm and steady like Dad's. "Actually, Nelson is Cuban American, Catalina is half Guatemalan, and you know what? I wish I could speak Spanish with them. I really do. But I'm taking French because my mother wanted me to."

Fay doesn't blink. "You're still grounded," she says. "You are not leaving this house until Monday."

Chapter Six

I stomp up to my bedroom, so angry at Fay that my breath comes in heaves. She has no right to decide how I should be punished. Dad is my parent, she's not. And how can she put him down like that? Nice to get some support *for once*? Who does she think she is?

There's nothing like getting mad to make you more determined. I'm going to do such a good job on my travel brochure that Dad will stand up to Fay and not let her ground me, so there.

I flip open my laptop, with its wallpaper of Adam Kessler in *Angel*. If he came to the Hunger Unmasked Ball and I was stuck sitting at home, I'd lose my mind. And having to miss trick-or-treating with the Vampire Prom Queens would be just as bad.

I take a deep breath, putting the ball and Halloween out of my head for the moment. Then I Google *French-speaking countries.* There are a lot more than I thought, in Europe, Asia, and Africa, not to mention the French parts of Canada. We went to Montréal once when I was little, but Québec isn't really a country.

I decide to do my travel brochure on Guadeloupe, a butterfly-shaped island in the Caribbean with active volcanoes and tropical rain forests. I read that the local cuisine is "a mixture of French and Indian flavors," which sounds delicious. There are photos of palm tree–lined beaches with aquamarine water, the exact color of Adam's eyes. Sign me up!

The thing is, I really like schoolwork when you get to do something halfway creative, like making a travel brochure. Why can't teachers give homework like this all the time instead of just making us memorize long lists of words for a test?

That night, I'm a model student. I do my geometry homework, fill in every blank on my social studies worksheet, and rewrite my essay on *Romeo and Juliet* with all of my teacher's corrections before I go back to my Guadeloupe research. The island's history is really cool — Columbus landed there in 1493, and it was a haven for *pirates*! Of the Caribbean! I get so into it that when Jess makes her nightly phone call, I tell her, "I really can't talk now. I'm doing my homework."

"Whoa," says Jess, very surprised. "Okay, I guess. See you tomorrow."

Guadeloupe's principal exports are bananas (*les bananes*) and sugarcane (*canne à sucre*). I draw pictures of both, and am making the front cover for my brochure when somebody knocks at my door. Steeling myself for Fay, I draw my bathrobe tighter around myself and say, "Come in."

But it's Dad. "I just wanted to wish you good night," he says.

"Okay," I say, nodding. "Good night."

I wait for him to say something more, but he doesn't. The silence between us speaks volumes. I wish I could beg him to reason with Fay, but I know he won't do that unless the decision is his. He's still upset with me over the tablecloth incident, and if I force him to take sides, I'm sure that he'll take Fay's again. The thought makes me sick to my stomach.

Dad looks down at the pile of homework on my bed, the pictures I've drawn, and the half-finished cover with C'EST GUADELOUPE written out in the colors of the French flag. "You're a good kid," he says softly.

But then he turns away, closing the door to my room. I hear his heavy footsteps padding downstairs, and turn back to my work.

This is not over yet.

Jess and I meet at the corner of Underhill Avenue on Friday morning. "It's all squared away for tonight," she reports as we hike up the hill. "Jason is getting a ride to my house and my mom's going to drive all four of us — we'll stop at Will's house on the way. So you just have to get to my house before seven so we can get into our costumes."

"There's only one problem," I tell her.

"What?"

"I'm kind of grounded."

Jess stops in her tracks. "You're *what*? Are you kidding?"

"I wish. Fay grounded me until Monday."

"On Halloween weekend? That is so mean! Is that why you were drowning in homework last night?"

85

"Exactly. I'm hoping my dad will take pity on me if I work really hard."

"And what if he doesn't?" Jess asks.

I just shake my head. There's a plan forming inside my brain, but I'm not quite ready to go there. Not yet. "I don't know," I tell Jess.

"But you have to come with us. You *have* to!" Jess sounds totally frantic. That makes two of us.

The day before a holiday weekend is always a litmus test for teacher coolness. In some classrooms, tense teachers strain to make their checked-out class pay attention. Others are happy to go with the holiday flow, and throw parties, serve snacks, and show movies in class.

Madame Lefkowitz is not one of those teachers. "*Le Halloween n'est PAH célébré en France,*" she declares, so even though we just came from a class where the teacher was wearing a skeleton necklace and showed *The Nightmare Before Christmas*, we have to do grammar exercises. I'm still doing my best to be Little Miss Perfect, so I'm the only one raising my hand. It feels very strange.

Whenever I find a free minute, I'm working away on my travel brochure. "What is that thing you've been coloring all day long?" Sara asks me at lunch as everyone trades Reese's Pieces and candy corn.

"It's about Guadeloupe," I say. "Project for French."

"Did you write about zouk?" asks Will from down the table.

"Zouk?" laughs Amelia. "What's zouk?"

"It's this really cool music, kind of like reggae, but in French," says Will. "I could burn you a CD if you want."

"That would be awesome," I say, and he smiles at me in a way that makes my whole face feel warm.

"So we're all systems go for tonight," says Amelia between bites of hot dog. She always buys her lunch at school, since her mom hates to cook. "I'll be working the door, and I'll have my phone on me, so text me as soon as you get there. I'll let you know if the coast is clear."

I'm about to tell her that I'm grounded when Ethan stops by. He puts both hands on the table, leaning toward me and Jess. His expression is pure disbelief. "Kayleigh just told me you two made my *costume*?"

"True fact, clown-boy," Jess says with a smirk. "I did your incredibly excellent mask, and Diana here made your appropriate jester hat."

Ethan groans, clutching his chest. "Oh, man, that is painful. I might have to leave that mask home tonight."

"Don't you *dare*!" says Jess. "If you want to leave something home, try leaving Kayleigh."

"You're *so* jealous, Munson. You totally like me," grins Ethan.

Jess picks up a lunch bag. "Excuse me, I have to throw up now."

"Oh, very mature," Ethan says.

"Must have learned that from you," Jess snaps back, and Amelia and Sara say, "Burn!" at the same time, like they've been rehearsing it.

I love my friends.

Work is fun, too, and almost helps me forget my worries. Chris the maintenance man has hung Halloween cutouts and black and orange streamers across the front window, and someone — not Joyless, I'm sure — has put big bowls of Snickers and Kit Kat bars out on the customer counter.

Dad is wearing a jeweled plastic crown that looks just like the neon sign on the window. He might be the king, but I'm feeling more like the scullery maid than the princess. For once in my life, I don't seize the excuse to dress up. But Cat comes to work wearing cat ears.

"What else?" she says, grinning.

MacInerny and Lara are not wearing costumes, of course, but as Cat points out while we're working together, they don't really have to. "Both of them go as ogres every day," she says with a smirk, and I couldn't agree with her more.

At the end of the workday, just before I'm about to head home, Nelson calls me up front to the Tailoring section. Loretta and Sadie are both wearing Halloween sweatshirts — Loretta's is black with orange pumpkins and Sadie's is orange with black cats — but Nelson is dressed the way he always dresses, plus a funny pair of red horns on his head.

"Halloween presents for you and the redhead," he says, handing me a bright orange paper bag. "For your Vampire Prom gowns."

Should I tell him I won't get to go trick-or-treating? I can't bear to, especially not when he's brought me a gift.

I reach into the bag and pull out two long satin sashes, like the ones Miss America winners wear over one shoulder. One of them says MISS TYPE A and the other says MISS CONGENIALITY (O NEGATIVE).

"Those are hysterical," I tell him. "Thank you so much."

Nelson studies my face. "What's the matter?"

How does he know me so well? "Nothing," I say.

"I don't buy it," he says. "You can't fake me out. I'm the king of the fakers. You might as well tell me what's wrong."

He folds his arms, waiting, and everything I've been holding back pours out in a rush. "My stepmother grounded me. I'm not allowed to go trick-or-treating tomorrow. Or to the masquerade ball tonight."

Nelson just shrugs. "So? 'Not allowed' never stopped you before."

For a minute, I'm taken aback, and then I realize . . . he's right. I think about the past two months. I wasn't allowed to go to *Angel* either, and I had the time of my life. I sneaked into the Foreman Academy dressed in a uniform that wasn't mine, and made a whole bunch of new friends.

And if I hadn't bent a few rules, I would certainly not have been cast in a Tasha Kane video. It's not like I'm *trying* to lie to Dad and Fay. It's just that it's hard to be thirteen years old when the world is so full of adventures, and everyone's telling you no.

The last piece of the plan I've been forming clicks into place. "Thanks," I tell Nelson. "Nice horns, by the way."

"*Muchas gracias*," he says with a wink. "Have fun tonight."

The house is in total chaos when Dad and I come through the kitchen door. Both twins are rocketing up and down the stairs, screaming, "Mo-om! I can't find my sleeping bag!" and "Where's my pajama top?"

"In the laundry basket on top of your bed!" Fay shouts back up the stairs. "And your sleeping bags are already down here! I *told* you!"

She turns back toward Dad, who's hanging his coat in the closet. "Go get your suit on. We have to get going!" Fay is wearing a violet cocktail dress, rhinestones, and shimmery stockings, but her feet are in plaid bedroom slippers, which makes her look a little ridiculous. Her high heels sit on top of the boot bench, next to two pink sleeping bags and a gift wrapped in Bratz wrapping paper and labeled MARISSA. Fay must be planning to drop off the twins at their sleepover party on the way to this dinner with her office friends, and it sounds like they're already running late.

Perfect. I'll have the whole house to myself, with no witnesses. I swallow my nerves, doing my best to look sorry for myself, like I would if I really were stuck here at home all night long.

Dad sighs and heads up the stairs as Fay shouts, "Girls! Remember your toothbrushes!"

Ashley is the first one downstairs. She's stuffed about six outfits into her *High School Musical* backpack, so it looks like a sausage about to split open its casing. "You smell like dry cleaning," she greets me. She says this at least three or four times a week, and each time she acts like it's news.

"Hello to you, too," I tell her as Brynna lumps down the stairs, dragging her Tasha Kane backpack behind her. It isn't as full as Ashley's, but there's a big bulge on one side that must be a stuffed animal. I don't know if it's pathetic or sweet that she still takes stuffed animals with her on sleepovers. Probably a little of both.

"You can microwave one of those frozen burritos," Fay tells me as she hands Ashley her parka. "Or heat up some soup. There's black bean, chicken noodle, and split pea with ham."

"I'll be fine," I say, stepping aside so Brynna can get to her coat. Inside my head, I'm gloating. I'll be a lot more than just "fine."

Dad appears at the top of the stairs, threading a belt through the loops of his old black suit pants. "I should have asked Nelson to let out this waistband," he grumbles. "I feel like I just ate a Thanksgiving dinner. Have you got the rest of our —"

Fay lifts up a shopping bag. "Hurry," she says. "I'll go warm up the car." She picks up Marissa's gift and goes out. Ashley and Brynna trail after her, carrying backpacks and sleeping bags. Neither of them says good-bye to me. I could call "Have fun!" after their backs, but it might sound sarcastic.

Dad and I look at each other. "I hate to think of you staying here all by yourself," he says. "We'll probably be out until midnight."

"I'll be fine," I say again in a brave, make-the-best-of-it voice that should win an Oscar. "If I get all that extra homework done tonight, and do chores tomorrow, maybe you'll change your mind about letting me go trick-or-treating tomorrow night."

"Don't get your hopes up," says Dad, pulling his coat back on over his suit jacket.

"I know," I say, reaching to straighten his bow tie.

"If you need anything, the Wheelers are right next door." He gives me a kiss on the top of my head, then pats the coat pocket where he keeps his cell phone. "I'll check in on you from the restaurant, okay?"

Oops. I didn't think of *that*. I nod nervously.

"Bye, honey," Dad says. He looks sorry to leave.

"Bye," I tell him as Fay honks the horn of her idling SUV.

Dad says, "I better get going. Don't stay up too late."

As soon as the door shuts behind him, I snap into action. I charge up the stairs to my bedroom and comb my accessory wall, grabbing every piece of jewelry Jess or I might want to wear with our masquerade costumes and stuffing them into my purse.

94

My next stop is the kitchen, where I pop a frozen burrito into the microwave and turn on the timer. Then I carry my school backpack into the dining room, where I put the finished Guadeloupe brochure on the table and surround it with Internet printouts and research books. I unpack my colored pencil set and leave a few near the brochure, so it looks like I just finished working on it. I even add a pencil sharpener for added realism. It's like setting the props for a play. For good measure, I pile up my finished math worksheet, the *Romeo and Juliet* essay I wrote last night, and a couple of textbooks.

Just as I finish setting the stage for my "evening at home," the microwave dings. I head into the kitchen and take out the burrito, crumpling its wrapper and leaving it right in plain sight on top of the garbage. I take a deep breath, trying to keep myself calm. I'm kind of enjoying this sneaking around — it feels like I'm playing a double agent in some spy movie, leaving a trail of false evidence.

The burrito smells great, and I don't want to waste it, so I roll it up in a napkin to eat on the way up to Jess's.

Have I thought of everything? All but the phone. That could wreck the whole plan. In a flash of inspiration, I grab a plate off the dish drainer, knocking it just enough sideways that it bumps the kitchen phone off of its cradle. I press down the TALK button and wait till I hear the familiar "If you'd like to make a call" recording turn into fast beeps. If Dad can't get through on the landline, he's certain to try my cell, which I'm taking with me.

Feeling proud of myself for all my attention to detail, I head for the door. And pause with my hand on the knob.

The thing is, I'm not really a well-trained professional spy. I'm an eighth grader who's leaving her house after dark when she's supposed to be grounded. My heart's beating too fast, and I'm not sure whether it's from the excitement of getting to go to the masquerade ball, or the fear that I'm about to do something I know in my heart isn't right. Should I back down and actually *be* the good girl I've been playing?

But what if I did skip the ball, just to stay on the safe side, and Fay didn't relent about making me miss trick-or-treating as well? I'd lose my whole weekend. That isn't right either.

Thinking about Fay and how unfair she's being is just what I needed to push myself out the front door. As soon as I'm out in the cool evening air, with the twinkling lights of my neighborhood all around me and the Wheelers' inflatable Frankenstein grinning next door, I feel ready for anything.

It's going to be an incredible night.

Chapter Seven

My heart is still pumping when I ring the doorbell at Jess's house. I hear footsteps tumbling downstairs and the door is jerked open by her brother, Dash, with an ax in his head, spurting blood as he staggers. Of course I scream, and of course I'm embarrassed a split second later when I figure out it's a Halloween gag mask.

"Got you!" he cackles.

"That is so gross!" I say.

"Isn't it sick?" Dash squeezes a plastic bulb in his hand. It's attached to a tube that makes fake blood seep under the clear plastic mask on his forehead. "I totally got you, admit it!"

"You are so *lame*!" Jess shouts from upstairs, and her mother calls from the kitchen, "You two leave each other alone," in a voice that sounds as if she's been saying this all evening long. Which she probably has.

Mrs. Munson comes out of the kitchen and gives me a tired-looking smile. "Hi, Diana," she says. "Have you eaten dinner? We had chicken pot pie, and there's plenty left."

"I just had a burrito," I tell her, wishing I hadn't eaten it quite so fast. "But thanks very much."

"Come on up," yells Jess, and I head up the stairs to her room. My pink gown is hung on the back of the door, and our gorgeous masks sit side by side on the bed. My gloves and tiara are next to Will's mask. Jess is already wearing her mermaid gown, and her bouncy red curls are all flattened out under something that looks like the toe of a giant's sheer stocking. I hardly recognize her.

"What's with the bald cap?"

"You'll see in a minute," Jess says gleefully, tucking a stray wisp of hair into place with a bobby pin. "But put on your dress. We don't have much time."

I don't need any more prompting to peel off my peacoat and hoodie and jeans and get into that magical gown. With the darts and tucks Nelson taught me to make in the seams, it fits me like a dream. I head for the mirror to put on my tiara. The gown's long skirt trails on the floor and I suddenly realize what I forgot.

"Shoes!" I exclaim. "I can't wear this dress with my high-tops!"

"Oh, shoot," says Jess. "I'd offer you some of mine, but . . ."

". . . you've got munchkin feet," I finish. Jess is petite, and she always makes fun of my giant-size (I would say normal-size) feet.

"Mom?" Jess yells. "Can Diana try on your black shoes? She forgot hers."

Mrs. Munson comes up the stairs, giving a light little knock as she pushes the door open. "I might have something," she says, looking me up and down. "What a beautiful dress! I don't recognize you two at all."

"That's cause I usually have hair," says Jess with a laugh. Mrs. Munson just shakes her head. "It isn't the hair. It's how teenaged you look."

"Mom?" says Jess, laying a hand on her arm. "News flash: We're teenagers."

"I know. It just happened so *fast*," Mrs. Munson says. "Let's find some shoes for you, tall Diana."

She brings me into her bedroom and opens the closet. Alongside several pairs of the practical white shoes she wears at her nursing job sit a pair of wool-felt clogs, some olive green Birkenstock sandals, and a sensible pair of black dress shoes with clunky square heels. "How about these?" she says, holding them up.

My heart sinks, but I try them on. They're my size, and they're certainly better than Converses with pink and green laces, but they look more PTA meeting than masquerade ball.

"Oh, wait," Mrs. Munson says suddenly, rummaging in the side of her closet. "I had to buy something for my niece's wedding last summer. They won't keep your toes very warm, but they might look nice with your dress."

She takes out a shoe box and opens the lid. I gasp. Inside are a pair of strappy gold sandals with tapering heels.

"Oh, wow!" I breathe. "Those are just *perfect*. Could I really borrow them?"

"Please," Mrs. Munson says. "I'll never wear them again. I spend too much time on my feet to mess around with high heels. I just hope they won't give you blisters."

I step into the sandals and instantly feel tall and elegant. "I *love* them," I say.

"Can you walk?"

I nod. That's something I got really good at onstage, and I love the way heels make you feel instantly different. "They're pretty comfortable, actually."

"Well, be my guest. They look great on you."

"Thank you so much, Mrs. Munson!" I say, and I can't resist hugging her. Wait till Jess sees me in these!

But when I get back to her room, I'm the one who's amazed. Jess is wearing a shimmering light blue wig made of something like Christmas tree tinsel. "Do you love it or what?" she says.

"It's fantastic!" I tell her. "Where did you *get* that?"

"Mom took me and Dash to the Halloween store at the mall," Jess explains. "She gave us each twenty dollars, and he bought that hideous ax-murder mask. I already had my whole costume, and the plastic fangs for tomorrow were cheap, so . . . Ta-da!" She strikes a mermaid pose. "I feel like Lady Gaga!"

"I totally love it! Hey, check out these shoes." I pull up my hemline to show her the gold heels.

"You got those from Nurse Birkenstock?" Jess looks astonished. "Oh, right, I remember. Mom wore them to my cousin Bethany's wedding. She complained about blisters all night. Don't forget about these."

She tosses me the stretchy black evening gloves that we got from the Drama Club closet, and I pull them on. They go all the way up to my elbows.

"Those are awesome!" says Jess.

"We're awesome," I say as we look at ourselves in the mirror. We're really transformed, and my worries morph into a nervous excitement. All that sneaking around and rule-breaking was worth it.

"We are," says Jess. "We're amazingly awesome."

She picks up her cell phone and snaps a quick photo of us in our finery. "We're supposed to text Amelia from outside the building," she says, slipping her phone in her purse. "Are you taking your phone?"

103

"Definitely. My dad might be calling me on it."

"That's right, I forgot to ask. How did you manage to get ungrounded?" Jess asks me.

I take a deep breath. "I didn't. Dad and Fay are out for the night, and so are the twins. I'm supposed to be home doing French."

Jess's eyes widen, and she lets out a low whistle. "Wow, you've got some nerve."

"Well, I did do the French," I say. "That part is true. I just couldn't bear to stay home by myself. Especially not after making these costumes."

"Plus Ethan's," laughs Jess. "I cannot wait to see him in that clown suit. And I've got your back if you need me."

I nod. Jess saved my skin when I rushed back home after *Angel*. We've bailed each other out of one scrape or another since we were in preschool.

"What's Jason wearing?" I ask. "Is he going to be the fourth Jonas for real?"

"It's a secret," says Jess. "A bunch of his friends from the Foreman Academy go to this event every year, and they really get into the costume thing."

Just then we hear the sound of a car pulling up right in front of the house. Jess rolls up the shade to look down from her window, and there's a silver convertible sitting outside the house. In the front are a boy and girl who look like they stepped right out of an Abercrombie ad. As we watch, a curly-haired figure in black with a billowing cape unfolds himself out of the tiny backseat.

"It's him!" Jess squeals, and she knocks on the windowpane.

Jason looks up. He has on a black Zorro mask with a little black mustache drawn over his lip, and he's wearing a sword that he must have borrowed from the Foreman Academy's fencing team. He sees Jess, waves, and drops into a courtly bow as the silver car's driver toots on its horn and drives off.

"OMG!" says Jess. "*Look* at him!" She grabs my hand, squeezing it hard as Jason waves to her and strides up the sidewalk.

"Great costume," I say, wondering what Will's vintage band tux will look like.

Suddenly Jess gasps and bolts out of her bedroom. "My *brother*!" She charges down the hall and runs for the stairs as the front door swings open. I get to the top of the staircase just in time to see Dash do another dramatic ax-murder death scene and get tackled from behind by a mad blue-haired mermaid.

"Nice ax in your head," grins Jason.

"That is the kid brother item," says Jess, pushing past Dash toward the door. "Just ignore it."

"Whoa," Jason says. "You've got blue hair!"

"It's natural," Jess says with a comical primp of her glittery wig.

"I can see that," says Jason. "Just like my mustache."

Jess laughs. They're so *comfortable* with each other. How do they do it? Ever since Will and I figured out we both like each other, we've been total geeks.

"Hi, Diana," says Jason. I wave and smile. Jess's mother comes into the hall, and Jason turns toward her, offering a handshake. "Hello, Mrs. Munson. Thank you so much for driving us."

"Of course." Mrs. Munson smiles and shakes his hand, charmed by his manners. "How are you, Jason?"

"Fine, thank you very much." He's almost *too* polite. Dash, on the other hand, has no such problem.

"Is your sword sharp?" he asks, poking it with his finger. "Could you stab someone with it, like maybe my sister?"

"It's a fencing foil. Blunt at the tip. See?" Jason shows Dash the rubber tip at the end. "How do you do that blood-spurting thing?"

Dash is only too happy to demonstrate. "Who does that wicked-cool Mazda belong to?" he asks as he squirts fake blood with a hand pump.

"My R.A.," Jason says, explaining when Dash looks blank, "Residential Advisor. Semi-grown-up who lives on my hall. He calls it his Batmobile."

"Cool beans," says Dash. "Is it fast?"

While they're doing boy talk, Mrs. Munson asks, "Girls, are you ready to go?"

"We just have to get our masks," Jess says, saying over her shoulder to Jason, "Be back in a second."

He nods and she rushes upstairs, grabbing my hand as she passes. I follow her into her room, where she shuts the door, leans against a poster of the real Jonas Brothers, and sighs, "He's *so* cute! I can't stand it!" She turns toward the poster and says, "Sorry, Nick. Sorry, Joe. Sorry, Kevin. 4-J is live and in person."

I laugh and pick up our masks. "Come on, crush girl!"

Jess sits in front next to her mother, and Jason keeps up a nonstop stream of chat as we drive through the streets to Will's house. It's not all that far — I've never been there before, but I figured he must live close by, since he rides his bike to the ShopRite where he works on Sundays. His house is a split-level ranch just like all the others in the neighborhood, but as we pull into the driveway, I notice three dummies with pumpkin heads sitting outside the garage. One has a toy ukulele, the second is holding a beat-up guitar case, and the third one is playing the bongos.

"Oh, I get it," says Jason. "Garage band."

"Pretty funny," says Jess, and I can't help smiling. I'm picturing Will and his brother Steve making those dummies, stuffing old towels and rags in the clothing and arranging their gloves so they'd look like they're playing their instruments.

"Do you think they heard us pull up?" Mrs. Munson asks.

"No clue," says Jess. "Go ring the doorbell, Diana."

"You do it." There go my cheeks. Insta-blush.

"Oh, come on, get over yourself! You're going with three of your friends to a dance. What is the problem?"

I don't know what I would tell her, but I don't have to answer, because the front door swings open and out comes Will. He's wearing a dark maroon tux with black satin lapels and stiff shoulders, a white shirt, a Western string tie, and cowboy boots. It's a slightly bizarre combination, but somehow it all works together: He looks super handsome. He waves good-bye to his father, who's standing just inside the front door, then walks out to the car.

"Hey," he says, clambering into the backseat beside me. "Great dress!"

"Thanks," I say, sliding over. "Great boots." I'm sandwiched between him and Jason, and putting our seat belts on is incredibly awkward. When I buckle my seat belt, Will and I bump elbows hard.

"Sorry," he mutters.

"So what are you going as, dude?" Jason asks.

"I guess I'm . . . kind of a rock 'n' roll outlaw," says Will.

"I love it!" says Jess. "Just like *Angel*."

Okay, now I really am blushing. It's a good thing it's dark out — I don't want anybody to see my face. Maybe I should put on my mask and be done with it. "Oh," I tell Will. "Here's the mask that I made for you."

I hand it to him, and he holds it up next to the window to catch the glow of the streetlights. "Oh, cool," he says. "I love the black and white checks."

"It reminded me of a guitar strap," I say.

"Uh-huh, I can see that," Will says, sounding pleased but self-conscious. "Thanks." We look at each other, and the silence would probably go on all night if it weren't for Jason, who never has nothing to say.

The masquerade ball is at DiCandido's Palace, a swanky catering hall that usually does proms and weddings. I've driven by it a hundred times — you can't miss the long row of bottom-lit sculptures and fountains in front — but I've never been inside. It looks very imposing, and the idea that Will and I don't have tickets seems suddenly scarier than it did before. I pull on my mask, and Will does the same. As Mrs. Munson turns into the driveway, I slip my phone out of my pocket and quietly text Amelia:

we r here!

In seconds, her answer comes back:

cool, just get in line

That sounds simple enough, but my palms are still sweaty. I look out the window. There are several town cars and limos grouped under the carriage entrance, and the couples emerging look very well dressed.

Jess's mother frowns. "Are you sure we're at the right place?" This is kind of a weird question, since there's a big HUNGER UNMASKED banner stretched over the entrance and people are all wearing masks with their evening clothes. But I think I know what she means: The party guests crossing the parking lot are all *adults*. Maybe we don't quite belong in this crowd.

Just then a group of masked girls in ballet costumes climbs out of a minivan parked right in front of us. We're all relieved to see that we won't be the only guests our age, though of course these must be the performers. I crane my neck, looking for Amelia's big sister, Zoe, but all I can see is a blur of powder blue tutus.

"So where are *their* dates?" Jason wisecracks as we watch them go past like a flock of birds, dangling their toe shoes from ribbons. "Maybe they're meeting a soccer team inside."

Jess laughs really hard, and I have the weird feeling that if someone else said that, she wouldn't think it was that funny. If Ethan had said it, in fact, she'd be mocking him. It's funny what crushes can do to your brain.

Mrs. Munson pulls up to the entrance, where a cluster of older teenagers is waiting outside, on a for-real red carpet. "I'll meet you right here at eleven o'clock," she says.

"Mom, that's too early!" Jess wheedles. "It goes until midnight!"

"But I don't," her mother says firmly. "Eleven it is. And if you're not outside, I'll come inside and get you, dressed just like this." She gestures to her jeans and sweatshirt. "If you want to leave earlier, call."

"Okay, fine," Jess sniffs, pulling her mask on and folding her arms. Even with glitter-blue hair, she's a feisty redhead.

"Thank you for driving, Mrs. Munson," says Jason, ever the gentleman.

Will and I chorus, "Yeah, thanks," and get out of the car next to Jason and Jess.

The four of us stand on the edge of the red carpet, feeling more than a little bit out of our league as more costumed grown-ups swirl past us. Though I have to admit, we look pretty sensational.

"What did Amelia tell you?" Jess asks me.

"She just said, 'Get in line,'" I reply.

"Piece of cake," Jason says, taking two big red tickets for him and Jess out of his wallet.

Will and I look at each other, and I get the sense we both have the same thought: *Easy for* you *to say*.

We head for the revolving front door. Jason swishes back his Zorro cape and bows to Jess, saying, "After you, Madame." She glides ahead and I have to admit that her mermaid tail looks pretty magnificent, no matter how much trouble I'm in for that tablecloth.

Now comes the hard part. Will and I look at each other.

"Ready?" he says, and I nod, with my heart pounding fast.

"Just act natural," I whisper to him. "Act like you *deserve* to get in."

He whispers back under his mask, "No sweat. I'm a rock 'n' roll outlaw, remember?" I can't help but smile.

We go through the revolving door right behind Jess and Jason, looking as confident as we can manage. There's a big entry hall with restrooms in one corner and a coat check staffed by two people in flamenco dance costumes, but luckily we were all smart enough to leave our coats in the car.

Amelia spots us right away. She's standing right next to the open door into the ballroom, tearing tickets in half. She's wearing a red and white peppermint striped satin dress that looks like some kind of dance costume, though seeing soccer-captain Amelia in *any* dress is enough of a shock. The sounds of an amplified dance band come out through the door, and Will looks excited.

"Must be Dreamcatcher," he says, and starts nodding his head to the beat.

There's an elegant Asian couple in front of us, and Amelia tears their red tickets, dropping them into a tall jar. The man standing next to her, in a Moorish-style costume and turban, bands their left wrists with red paper bracelets.

Will and I exchange looks, but Amelia is cool as a cucumber. "May I take your tickets, please?" she says to

114

Jason and Jess, as if she's never seen them before in her life. I notice she's standing a bit to one side, so her body is blocking the bracelet guy's view of the jar that the tickets go into. Smart girl!

Jason hands over their tickets. Amelia tears them and drops them into the jar, and they step ahead to the bracelet guy. "May I take your tickets, please?" she says in the same neutral voice. But as Will and I take a step toward her, a straight-backed bald man in an eye patch and green velvet cape strides up to Amelia and tells her, "Your mother needs you in the back. Right away." Then he turns toward us and says, "Tickets, please." My stomach drops into my shoes.

As Amelia steps out of his way — what else could she do? — she lifts up her cell phone in a way that's clearly intended to let me know I should text her as soon as I can.

Okay, so she's got a Plan B. But that won't rescue this moment.

The man in the eye patch is staring at us. Will digs through his jacket and pants pocket as if he's searching for tickets, and my improvisation skills kick into gear. "Your *coat* pocket, dear," I say in an annoyed, snooty voice that I hope sounds much older. I am wearing a mask, after all. "You left it inside the Mercedes."

"Oh, *yes*," says Will, getting it.

"Honestly," I sniff at him, turning my head toward the man in the eye patch. "We'll be back in a jiff." And I grab Will's arm, dragging him out of the line.

We sweep through the revolving door and come back out on the red carpet. "Now what?" says Will.

"Keep walking," I say. "He's got one good eye; he can see through the glass."

We head into the parking lot, which is luckily huge. As soon as we're out of sight of the door, I pull out my cell and start texting Amelia:

now what?

Will shakes his head, chuckling.

"What's funny?" I say. "We're out in the cold, and Amelia's not working the door, and who knows how we're going to get in without tickets, and — what?"

Will is laughing out loud now. "Who says 'in a jiff'?"

"The lady whose date left his coat in the car."

"The *Mercedes*," Will says, and I start laughing, too.

"Well, at least I said *something*."

"No, it was classic," says Will, and I realize we're having *fun* with each other, not being awkward at all. Maybe all we need is a nice disaster to loosen us up.

Just then my phone beeps, and I read Amelia's text:

service ent in back — meet u 5 min

"Service ent?" says Will, reading over my shoulder. "You mean like those tree guys in *Lord of the Rings*?"

"Service *entrance*," I grin, and we start for the back of the building. The evening air is cool, and I feel myself shiver.

"Are you cold?" asks Will. "Here. Take my jacket." Before I can protest, he's pulled it off, draping it over my shoulders.

"Now *you'll* freeze."

"I'm fine," he says. "Rock 'n' roll outlaws don't freeze. We're already too cool."

"If you say so," I smile as we walk toward the back of the building. The jacket does help. Maybe those padded shoulders give off extra heat.

"Mento?" asks Will, offering a roll. How did he know they're my favorite candy?

"I *love* those," I say, popping a mint in my mouth. "Thanks."

Will looks over at me. "How can you walk in those heels?"

"How can you walk in cowboy boots?" I shoot right back, and he shrugs.

"I'm from New Mexico. These are like sneakers down there."

"Do you ever miss Santa Fe?" I ask him. I'd almost forgotten that Will used to live there. That must be where he got that cute Western string tie. The slide part looks like Navajo silver.

"Sometimes. We had a great band there, me and my brother and these three other guys. But this is kind of, I guess . . . it's good, too."

That sounds a bit more like the mumbly Will Carson I know from school, but I still can't get over the change in him. Maybe wearing a mask makes him feel less shy. Or maybe we're just getting used to each other. In a good way.

"Service ent!" I point to a white door right ahead of us, marked SERVICE ENTRANCE.

"Oh, cool," says Will, and we walk right up to it.

"Now what?" he asks. "You think we should knock?"

"Well, Amelia did say five minutes."

"Okay."

So we stand there and wait. Now that we've stopped walking and talking, I start feeling kind of self-conscious all over again. Will shuffles his feet.

"What was it called?" I ask him. "The band you and Steve had in Santa Fe?"

"Oh. Flash Flood."

"Flash Flood? I like that," I tell him. "Do you have a T-shirt?"

"A T-shirt?" Will asks, looking blank.

"You know, how you always wear T-shirts with bands."

"No I don't."

I stare. "Are you kidding me? When was the last time you came to school wearing a T-shirt that didn't have some kind of band logo?"

"I don't look at my T-shirts, I just put them on."

119

That has got to be the most boy sentence I've ever heard. But before I can think of a response, the service entrance swings open.

"Come inside, quick," says Amelia, glancing over her shoulder. We do.

"Boy, am I glad to see *you*!" I tell her, handing Will's jacket back to him. He slips it back on as we follow Amelia down a long hallway, past broom closets and slop sinks.

"I checked out the whole layout beforehand, just as a backup," she says, looking pleased with herself. "I'm one-stop shopping for gate-crash technique. There's a door through the storeroom. Could you *believe* Zaloom's timing?"

"That bald guy? Who is he?" Will asks her.

"Ballet master. Head of Fleet Feet. Here, put these on, in case somebody sees you." She reaches into her sleeve and hands us two red paper bracelets.

I'm amazed. "How did you —"

"Stashed them before, just in case," Amelia says with a satisfied smirk. "What do you think, I'm an amateur?"

"You're all pro," I say, fastening the bracelet over my evening glove.

"Not when it comes to ballet, let me tell you. My mom's got me stuffed into this *Nutcracker* costume. I feel like an idiot." Amelia's leading us through a storeroom full of catering trays and supplies. There's a curtain in back, and we can hear amplified music coming from the other side. "Side door to the ballroom. You'll come out behind the buffet. I've got to get back to my post from the bathroom," she says, making air quotes on *bathroom*. "I'll check you guys later." And off she goes.

Will and I look at the curtain, then at each other. "You ready?" he says, and I nod, holding my breath as we push through.

We're inside!

Chapter Eight

The ballroom is enormous, with glittering chandeliers like something out of *Phantom*. Just as Amelia told us, we've entered through a side door behind a gigantic buffet table. Some of the cater-waiters look miffed, but we've both got on our red bracelets, so for all they know, we're just some guests who went out to the bathrooms and wandered back in through the wrong door by accident.

"Excuse me," I say in my snootiest, in-a-jiff voice as we sidle past the cater-waiters and onto the dance floor. Will's got his eye on the bandstand, checking out the musicians, but the first thing I want to do is find Jess and Jason.

This doesn't take long — not far from the big buffet table is a smaller one with a liquid-chocolate fountain and baskets of things to dip in it: strawberries, marshmallows, pretzels, grapes, and cubes of angel food cake. I'm not too surprised to see a blue-haired mermaid and Zorro standing right in front of it.

Jess spots me, too. I can see her eyes widen behind her mask. "How'd you get in?" she asks around a mouthful of chocolate-dipped pretzel. "That bald guy was *scary*."

"Amelia was awesome," I tell her. "Who knew she was so good at breaking and entering?"

"Oh, please," says Jess. "Do you know how many stadiums that girl has gate-crashed? She never buys tickets for anything if she can help it."

Funny the things you find out about people.

I look around the ballroom, drinking in all the sights. Along with the glamorous gowns and tuxedos, the elegant masks give everybody an aura of mystery. A few people must not have gotten the glamour memo, though, because they're wearing Halloween costumes like Elphaba from *Wicked* or Captain Jack Sparrow — I'm glad our mermaid and Zorro are not in this all by themselves. There's even a frizzy-haired man dressed like the Mad Hatter in *Alice in Wonderland*. I point him out to Jess.

"Hey! That guy stole my top hat!" she says.

"You own a top hat?" Jason sounds surprised, which just goes to show that he and Jess really don't know each other that well yet. Jess wears that top hat to school every day. I wonder what kinds of things she doesn't know about Jason. Right now, he's pointing out some of the kids he knows from the Foreman Academy. None of *them* missed the glamour memo — they're all decked out like extras from *Gossip Girl*. I remember the matching tall blond girls named Brooke and Mackenzie who tormented me and Jess not long ago, and I hope they're not in tonight's crowd.

It's nice to see more people close to our age, though. Except for the ballet school contingent and a few younger children who've come with their parents, the crowd seems much older than we are. But then I look back at my friends. In our borrowed finery, we don't look like thirteen-year-olds either. Maybe this room is chock-full of eighth graders, but we're all so fancy that no one can tell.

Jess scans the crowd with me. "How are we supposed to know who the guest stars are? They're all wearing masks."

"Maybe *we're* the guest stars," Jason says, and Jess grins.

"Amelia said they'll be getting here late, since they're sending a car to the city to pick them up after their shows," I remind her.

"You think they would take us along for the ride?" Jess asks. "That would be totally out of control. I bet they're going to send a stretch limo."

I flash back to the opening night of *Angel*, when Cat and I *did* get to ride in the back of a limo, driven by Nelson's uncle. The memory is a warm blur of leather seats, twinkle lights, music, and red taillights streaking through the Lincoln Tunnel. I still can't believe it was real. Or that I'm here in this ballroom, tonight.

"What do you think of the band?" I ask Will, who's been watching them since we came in. His head bobs to the beat and he sways very slightly.

"Not bad," he says. "Pretty tight horns. They could use a new bass player."

This makes me smile. "Like you?"

"No, he's better than I am. But when I'm his age I'll be better than him." He dips a marshmallow in the chocolate fountain, popping it into his mouth while it's still gooey. "Wow," he says. "That's *really* good."

I skewer a strawberry and hold it under the cascading chocolate, then pop it onto my tongue. It's delicious. The refreshments at parties I'm invited to are usually bowls of Doritos and Oreos, unless someone's mother goes on a health kick and loads up the table with hummus and vegetables no one but me ever eats.

But the food at this party goes on and on. There's a hot buffet line, a salad bar on ice, giant platters of cheese and fresh fruit. It seems kind of ironic, when this is supposed to raise money to fight against hunger, but I'm not about to complain. Not when there's a free chocolate fountain.

"Let's go attack that buffet," Jason says. "Check out that guy in the puffy white hat carving roast beef."

There is indeed a red-bearded man in a chef's hat and apron carving away at a roast, and guests are lined up with plates. There's something incredibly strange about seeing people eat roast beef and scalloped potatoes in ball gowns and masks. Some of the people wearing full-face masks have slid them up onto the top of their heads, with the elastics tucked under their chins so they look like kids' birthday hats.

I notice that each dish has a card from the restaurant

or catering service that donated it. That means every penny they're raising tonight will really go to fight hunger, which makes me feel suddenly super guilty about sneaking in. When I get my check from the Tasha Kane video, I'll make sure to send some of the money to Arts Against Hunger. Between that and the money I owe to Dad, my earnings won't last long. But it's worth every penny to be here tonight.

We all pile our plates high, though mine's a burrito less high than everyone else's, and retreat to a quiet corner. While we're eating, we watch people dancing and take votes on best and worst costumes. Everyone has different favorites, and I'm searching for mine when I spot a group coming through the door wearing outfits I'd recognize anywhere: the red-and-gold Carnivale costumes and masks Jess and I made with Nelson.

"Mall rat alert!" I say, pointing. "Kayleigh Carell has arrived."

Jess swivels and hoots. "Is that *Ethan*?"

"You bet," I tell her. Ethan's clown costume billows like parachute silk. The left arm and right leg are bright red, and the opposite gold. The neckline is layered with multiple ruffles, and with his chubby-cheeked mask and jester hat, he looks completely hilarious.

Will starts cracking up. "I can't believe Kayleigh got him to wear that."

"Who is Kayleigh?" asks Jason.

"Your basic Blake Lively wannabe mean blonde," I say, remembering Nelson's words. "You know Brooke and Mackenzie from Foreman? She's their public school clone." I point out Kayleigh, who's fluffing her hair in her red-and-gold shepherdess gown.

Jason lets out a whistle. "Whoa, scary. And Ethan?"

"Her boyfriend. The clown prince of dorks," says Jess, waving him over. "I am so going to torture him."

"How would he know who you are?" Jason asks. "You've got blue hair and fins."

"I told him that I was going to go as a mermaid, duh," Jess says, waving wider and calling, "Yo, Ethan! Nice mask!"

Ethan sees her and turns to nudge Kayleigh. Even from across the room I can read the dynamic: He wants to come join us, she doesn't. I can't wait for the moment she realizes that the girl in the pink gown and elegant mask is *me*, that

I made it here after all. But what if she asks me how? I can't tell the truth — she might squeal on Amelia. Then I get a wicked idea.

"Hey, guys, don't tell Kayleigh I'm me, okay?"

"Don't you think she's going to figure it out, since you're standing right next to me?" Jess asks.

"I'm two inches taller in these heels, I'm wearing a mask, and Kayleigh knows perfectly well that I couldn't afford to buy tickets," I remind her. "Besides, she's in Kayleigh World. Other people don't really register."

Will bursts out laughing. "I'm in," he says. "I want to prank Ethan."

"Tell them we're some of your friends from the Foreman Academy," I hiss to Jason as Ethan and Kayleigh come over.

"Hey, Munson, you look like the catch of the day at the Stop and Shop fish counter," Ethan says.

"Who *is* this clown?" Jason wisecracks.

Jess shrugs, "He goes to my school. Unfortunately."

"The feeling is mutual," Ethan says. "Very. You must be that guy from the Foreman Academy. Jason, right?"

"That's right," Jason says. "Who are you?"

"Bozo the Magnificent, aka Ethan Horowitz. This is Kayleigh Carell."

"Hello, Kayleigh," says Jason with full-tilt charm. "My name is Jason."

"Hi, Jason," she simpers. "So you go to Foreman?"

"Who doesn't?" I say in my haughtiest accent.

Jason says, "Oh. This is Taylor, and —"

"*Taylor,*" I drawl, looking over at Will. Kayleigh looks at him, too.

"You're *both* named Taylor?" she asks with a giggle. "That is, like, crazy!"

I shrug, enjoying this. "Taylor Lautner went out with Taylor Swift, right? It's a Taylor thing." I nudge Will in the ribs. "Right, Taylor?"

"For sure," Will says in a preppy-toned voice that's so far from his own that I want to hug him. Who knew he could improvise? I'm finding out lots of cool things about Will tonight.

Ethan's head swivels from Will to me, then back to Will. Even with a mask on, I can see his eyes light up as he figures it out. Will *is* his best friend, after all — it makes sense that Ethan would recognize him even through a disguise. I hold my breath, waiting for Ethan to unmask us, but he decides to play along with the game.

"So," he says, grinning. "Taylor and Taylor. You must be tailor-made for each other."

"Oh, vomit," groans Jess.

"All over your outfit," says Ethan. "Speaking of fish, how's the food at this joint?"

"Four-star," Jason says before Jess can answer. "There's a chocolate fountain."

"Oh, wow!" exclaims Kayleigh.

"I had one of those at my birthday," I say in been-there, done-that Taylor tones. "In Switzerland."

"Really?" says Jess, pretending she's very impressed. "That is so cool, Taylor! What were you doing in Switzerland?"

"My parents have a ski condo in . . ." Suddenly I go blank. I can't think of a single city in Switzerland. "In the Swiss Alps."

"In Gstaad," Jason says smoothly, flashing a grin. "Near Château d'Oex." His French accent is perfect. I picture my French brochure on the dining room table, alone in a house with the phone off the hook, and feel a small stab of guilt.

131

"That sounds terrific," gushes Kayleigh, her hand going up to her long blond hair. "So do you love going to Foreman or what? I heard it's, like, excellent."

"You'd fit right in," Jason says, and I practically lose it. She would!

The evening continues in a happy blur. We eat and talk, check out the weird artwork for sale at the silent auction, and make tons of Taylor jokes. Kayleigh is clueless. At one point Amelia comes up from behind in her peppermint stripe dress, off duty. "Hi, guys," she says, "Are we having fun yet?"

My blood pressure goes through the roof. I signal to her behind Kayleigh's back, shaking my head no and drawing a finger across my throat. Jess jumps in, saving the day. "We're having a blast," she says quickly. "Have you met Taylor and Taylor? We call them Tayloraylor. Kind of like Brangelina."

"Taylor and Taylor?" Amelia says, raising her eyebrows. "Hi, I'm Amelia. Kind of like Amelia Bedelia." She shakes our hands solemnly. Somehow we all manage to keep a straight face.

"Great dress, BTW," Jess says. "Where did you get it?"

"Oh. Fleet Feet does the *Nutcracker Suite* every year, and they wanted the volunteers to dress in the costumes. I wanted to go as the Mouse King, but Zaloom wouldn't let me."

"Who is Zaloom?" Jason asks. As Amelia is fills him in on Mikhail Zaloom, the half-Russian, half-Persian head of Fleet Feet, I look over at Kayleigh, who's still totally clueless. I almost feel sorry for her. But just as I start to relax and enjoy being Taylor the snob from the Foreman Academy, my cell phone goes off. My blood pressure spikes right back up. It's got to be Dad.

"I can't hear a *thing* in this room," I say in Taylor's voice as I step toward the drapes at the back of the ballroom and answer the phone in my own voice. "Hello?"

"Diana?" says Dad. "I've been calling and calling. What's wrong with the landline?"

"I don't know," I say. "I was talking to Jess a few minutes ago. Maybe I forgot to hang it back up."

"Well, I'm glad you're all right. What's that music?"

Oh, no. "Just my iTunes," I say, with a wince at the lie. "It's so loud."

133

"Let me turn it down," I say, stepping behind a tall velvet drape. "Better?"

"A little."

"Where are you calling from, Dad? I hear traffic."

"I stepped outside the restaurant," he says. "We're just finishing dinner with Fay's friends from work. I wish I could come right back home, but Fay is dead set on attending this party and I promised her I would put in an appearance."

Thank goodness they're not going home yet!

"I'm fine," I assure him. "There's no need to rush. I'll be fast asleep by the time you get back."

"I love you, Diana," says Dad, and I feel like a terrible person.

"I love you, too, Dad," I say. At least that part's the truth.

Feeling shaky, I hang up and go back to my friends. Amelia is still going on about Mikhail Zaloom. "Ego the size of the *moon*," she says. "Totally arrogant. Uh-oh. Speaking of which . . ."

She points at the bandstand, where the musicians are putting their instruments down for a break. The man with

the green cape and eye patch has stepped up to the microphone, along with a cherry-wigged woman who's wearing
a gingerbread-patterned hoopskirt.

"Amelia?" asks Jess. "Am I nuts, or is that —"

"My mother, the ex-ballerina. It is. Can I sink through
the floor now?"

"Greetings, revelers," says Mikhail Zaloom in an echo-
ing voice that sounds like the narrator of some very dull
PBS documentary. His bald head shines under the spotlight. "With apologies to Herr Drosselmeier," he says,
flipping his eye patch up onto his forehead and putting on
round horn-rim glasses, "I should like to be able to read
my remarks."

An obedient ripple of laughter stirs through the crowd.
I hear a man whisper behind us, "Don't do us any favors,"
followed by a laughing, hissed "Shh!"

The couple behind us must know this Zaloom guy
pretty well, because sure enough, he makes an extremely
long speech, singing the praises of Arts Against Hunger and
thanking dozens of benefit sponsors by name. Finally the
guy behind us says impatiently, "Oh, just get on with it,
will you?"

His voice is a little too loud, and his wife hisses "Shh!" again, louder this time.

I'm with him.

At long last, Zaloom finishes speaking and takes a hammy bow. The audience applauds, though it's not clear whether they're clapping for him or just glad that he finally shut up. He turns the microphone over to Amelia's mom, who gives an airy wave to the crowd and says, "I'll be brief."

The heckler behind us whispers, "That'll be different!" and his wife says, "Cut it *out*, Manny."

"I want to urge all of you to come out and see the Fleet Feet *Nutcracker* this holiday season," Mrs. Williams smiles. "You'll get a sneak preview of the snowflake dancers tonight, along with some wonderful songs by our surprise guest Broadway stars, who will be here as soon as they've taken their bows in that *other* arts capital across the river, Manhattan."

"She makes that same joke every time," says Amelia, rolling her eyes.

"So relax and enjoy!" says her mother. She drops into a theatrical curtsy.

The crowd claps again, she signals for music, and somebody turns on the sound system. The music is lush and romantic — it's Beyoncé's cover of the classic oldie "At Last." All around the room, couples come onto the dance floor.

"May I?" says Jason to Jess, and she nods, looking nervous but thrilled. He holds out his hand, and they start dancing together, not super close, but a definite pair. So do Ethan and Kayleigh. Will and I look at each other, both of us tongue-tied.

"You want to?" I finally ask him.

Will looks at his feet. "I'm not much of a dancer."

"Is Taylor?"

He laughs at that. "I don't know. Maybe."

I'm not sure how I find the nerve, but I hold out one evening-gloved hand and Will takes it. We don't stand too close, but it's nice just to move to the music together. I study Will's face through the eyeholes of my lace-trimmed black mask. He's got a mask on as well, but I get a good view of his eyes, which are shiny and dark, like Johnny Depp's.

He's not really looking at me, though, more over my

137

shoulder, and seems pretty stiff and uncomfortable. For a musician, he's very uptight about dancing . . . or maybe it's just about dancing with *me*. It's that not-quite-going-out-with-each-other thing, driving us crazy as usual.

Well, couldn't we just dance as *friends*? I mean, Jess and Amelia and Sara and I dance together all the time. It's not a big deal, right?

But as soon as Will and I start to relax just a little, a young guy in a black opera cloak, white tie, and *Phantom of the Opera* mask taps on my shoulder. "May I cut in?" he asks with a smile. Who is he, one of those kids from the Foreman Academy? I shake my head quickly, turning back to Will. Then I notice a woman in white changing partners a few feet away, and look back at the masked guy again. The molded Phantom mask covers a bit more than half of his face, but something about the other half seems familiar.

Since Will seems relieved to stop dancing, I nod and say, "Sure."

"Thank you," the guy says, and his voice sounds a little familiar, too. He whirls me into a turn. His movements are confident, practiced. Whoever this Phantom is, he's a *very* good dancer. He looks at my face with a smile on his lips.

"That's a beautiful gown," he says. "Where did you find it?"

If only he knew!

"Oh. I picked it up right here in town," I say quickly.

"I bet you did," he says, sounding amused.

Why does he think I'm so funny, and why do I feel like I *know* his voice? Where have I heard it before? I look into his eyes as he spins me around, and a memory starts to seep through . . . of us dancing, just like this, but under the stars. . . .

"You got taller again. But you aren't English tonight," says the mystery guy, and I nearly faint.

It's *Adam Kessler*!

Chapter Nine

"How did you recognize me?" I gasp. My heart's turning cartwheels. It's all I can do not to fall on the floor.

Adam shrugs, looking pleased with himself. "I know you live in Weehawken, remember? Not 'Wimpole Street, London,' like you told me on opening night." He flashes another smile. "I thought you might come to an evening like this. Anyway, you look just like yourself with a mask on."

Not to Kayleigh, apparently. But Adam looks just like himself with a mask on, too, and those gorgeous blue eyes are hypnotic. I'm dancing with the face on my computer.

Oh. My. God. How amazing is this?

"I was hoping you'd be here," I blurt, and immediately feel like a total dork. I better say something else fast. "Why aren't you wearing your costume from *Angel*?"

"You mean the bandanna, duster, and chaps? Doesn't feel very 'masquerade ball,'" Adam says with a grin. "So I borrowed this one from a friend."

My eyes open wide. "You mean . . . ?"

"The *Phantom* theatre is right down the street, and my friend understudies the lead. We all hang out in the same café after our curtain calls."

A Broadway café after curtain calls? That sounds like heaven on earth.

So is dancing with Adam. There's a reason the word for some people is *star*. Being with them is like looking up at the sky. It's dizzy and thrilling, and makes you feel millions of miles from the rest of your life.

"So what's new at the world's coolest dry cleaners?" Adam asks, breaking the spell. "And who was that guy in the hip checkered mask? Should I let you get back to him?" I look around with a guilty start, realizing that I forgot all about Will.

"That's my friend Will," I say hastily, stressing the "friend" part a little too hard. "He doesn't like dancing that much."

Adam nods. "Is he an actor?"

141

"Not usually." Should I tell Adam about our Taylor and Taylor charade? Would he think it was funny, or just immature? I decide not to mention it.

"How is your leading lady?" I ask in what I hope can pass for a casual tone.

"Sigrid? We came in the same car." I bet they did. I've read rumors on Broadway blogs that they're dating, though she was with another guy at the opening gala.

Adam cranes his neck, scanning the dance floor. "She's wearing her costume from *Angel*, so she should be easy to spot. . . . There she is!"

I follow his gaze, and spot Sigrid Wilner through the crowd. She has on a white mask with ribbons and the ruffled white dressing gown that I remember from their love duet. I've played the sound track about six hundred times, and that song always makes me swoon.

I look back at Adam. The light from the chandelier hits his eyes perfectly and I practically swoon for real. It's an entirely different feeling than I get when I'm with Will — it's deliciously fizzy and just a bit dangerous. Is it just because Adam's a celebrity? But if this is only some starstruck crush, why does fate keep on throwing the two of us together on dance floors?

And why did it give him that voice and those eyes?

This is all so *confusing*.

But magical. You can't deny that, and I wouldn't want to. My heart doesn't flutter like this when I'm dancing with Will.

I'm sad when the song comes to an end. "That was fun," Adam says with a smile. "Will you introduce me to your friends?"

Oh, help! Could this be any more awkward? Now I'll have to let him in on the whole Taylor story, or else blow my cover with Kayleigh. That would be just too embarrassing.

"The benefit planners want us to mingle with fans," Adam adds, which might sound a little conceited if he didn't say it in a charming, can-you-believe-this-silliness? way.

Well, Jess will love meeting him anyway. She really *is* a fan.

"Um, sure," I tell Adam. "But I'm 'Taylor' tonight."

"Of course you are," he says with a laugh. "Are you ever yourself?"

Now there's a good question.

We thread our way back through the crowd to where my friends have gathered, and I roll out my best Taylor attitude. "Everyone? Meet Adam Kessler."

Jess takes one look at his Phantom costume and says, "Oh, you are *not*." Adam turns toward her and flips up his mask, and she screams so loud I have to put a gloved hand over her mouth. Even so, people are turning to look at us.

Jess jumps up and down with excitement. "I loved, loved, loved *Angel*," she gushes. "Adored it!"

Kayleigh chimes in. "You're in *Angel*?" Her eyes open wide. "OMG, you're *him*! You're that guy in the ads! I read about you in *J-14*!"

Adam nods sheepishly, grinning as both of them bubble and squeal, and I get the feeling that he's gotten used to this kind of reaction from girls. Me included.

I look over at Will, who is studying the toes of his cowboy boots. Ethan and Jason both look a bit grumpy.

"How do you two know each other?" asks Jason.

"Oh, Taylor and I go way back. We did a show together not long ago," Adam says with a mischievous grin.

"Really?" Kayleigh turns to me, breathless. "What was it?"

"It was . . . a performance piece. Kind of an improvised thing," I reply.

Adam laughs. "You can say that again. It was fun-filled and action-packed. We called it *Opening Night*."

Kayleigh giggles and beams at him, touching her hair. "It sounds fabulous."

"Aren't you supposed to perform here?" Ethan asks in a voice that's just shy of rude. I guess he's annoyed at the way Kayleigh's flirting with the Broadway star.

"Yes, they'll be trotting us out for a number, I think," Adam says.

"I can't *wait* to see it," Kayleigh flutters. "You know, I'm an actress, too."

Jess coughs very loudly. "*Excuse* me," she says. "There's a frog in my throat."

"Let me help you," says Ethan, and whacks her across the back.

"Hey!" says Jess.

"Heimlich maneuver," says Ethan, and whacks her again. Jess whacks him back this time.

"Heimlich you!"

"Stop it, you two!" Kayleigh says. "That is *so* immature."

I look over at Will to see if he's enjoying their exchange as much as I am. His mouth's a straight line. "Will?" I ask quietly.

"Don't you mean Taylor?" he says.

"What's the matter?" I whisper.

"Nothing," he says, but he doesn't look happy. Am I imagining it, or is Will Carson *jealous*? When he couldn't wait to stop dancing with me? I'm sorry, but that doesn't even make sense.

Adam raises a hand and waves someone over. "Sigrid!" he calls.

Jess's eyes nearly bug out of her head. "Sigrid *Wilner*?" she says. "You mean Angel herself? I don't believe this! I am so glad we came!"

Sigrid threads her way through the crowd and comes over to meet us. "Who are your friends, Adam?"

"I totally loved you in *Angel*," says Jess. "Your song, when you're wearing that same dress, it just broke my heart."

"Thank you," says Sigrid. "How sweet!"

Adam puts a hand on my shoulder, telling her, "And here is another costar from a long time ago. This is Taylor."

"Nice to meet you," I say, doing my best not to gush like Diana — Adam has his hand *on my shoulder*! — since I'm supposed to be seen-it-all, done-it-all Taylor. "Great show. Wish you well with it."

Adam continues, "And Taylor's friend —" He turns to where Will was standing, breaking off when he sees that there's nobody there.

I look around wildly. Where did Will go? Did he really stomp off in a jealous huff because I danced with Adam? That's completely ridiculous. Is he a toddler who has to go off in a corner and sulk?

I spot the maroon of his jacket. Will's threading his way through the crowd toward the door, and he doesn't look mad, just unhappy. I don't dare call his name; he's supposed to be Taylor, and anyway, the music and crowd sound would drown me right out. But now I feel sort of guilty.

"Excuse me," I say, and go after him, dodging between the Mad Hatter and two girls in sapphire blue gowns. There's a cluster of people around the front door. An elderly couple is saying good-bye to their friends as they leave for the night, and a handful of latecomers are handing their tickets to one of the *Nutcracker*-dressed volunteers.

Will jams his hands deep into his pockets and slumps past the ticket jar just as the turbaned guy fastens an entry bracelet on a woman wearing a Renaissance Faire lace-up gown. As she joins her husband, who is wearing a green feathered hat, I get a good look at the woman who's standing behind her in line. She's wearing a silver half mask and a violet cocktail dress, and my heart nearly stops in my chest.

It's . . . *Fay*!

I'm in so many flavors of trouble I can't even breathe. I'm supposed to be *grounded*, and here I am out at a glittering charity ball without a ticket, wearing a dress that I took from Dad's cleaners. Oh, and PS, Will is walking away. It's a good thing I'm wearing a mask, because my face must look like a sheet.

Fay joins the Renaissance Faire–looking couple, who must be her colleagues from work. I turn away fast so she won't see me, but I sneak a worried look over my shoulder. It's just the three of them so far. If Dad got his way and went home after dinner, my goose is already cooked.

If he didn't, he must be here, too, and he's bound to recognize me, mask or no mask — he might even recognize what I'm wearing, if he ever spotted this dress on the No Pickup rack. Dad is notoriously fashion-blind, but a satin pink gown is hard to miss. And what about Jess? She's got a wig on, at least, but the tail of her dress is made out of a customer's tablecloth! Even with green mesh and sequins sewn over most of the fabric, it might catch Dad's eye.

In a panic, I scuttle away from the door and rejoin my friends. The band's started playing a livelier song, and Adam is dancing with starry-eyed Kayleigh while Sigrid whirls Ethan around in his clown suit.

Jess takes one look at my face and knows something is wrong, but she probably assumes that it's Will. So she's totally thrown for a loop when I beg Jason urgently, "Can I borrow your cape?"

"I guess," he says, slipping it off his shoulders. "Are you cold or something?"

"Or something," I say, quickly retying the billowing cape. It doesn't quite cover my dress, but it helps. "My stepmother just walked through the door."

"No way!" says Jess. Even through her mask, I can see her eyes widen. She turns to look over my shoulder. "What is she wearing?"

"Silver mask, purple dress . . ."

"Oh, man," says Jess. "That's Fay, all right. You better hide."

"Is my father with her?"

Jess shakes her head. "She's standing with some kind of Robin Hood and Maid Marian duo. Oh, wait, there he is! He's giving a coat check tag to Robin Hood."

I don't dare to turn, but I crane my neck, peeking over one shoulder. Then my heart does a drum solo. That's undeniably Dad, in his black wedding suit and the same Halloween crown he wore at the cleaners, plus a silver half mask just like Fay's.

"Cover your tail!" I hiss.

"What?" says Jess, startled.

"Tablecloth from the cleaners. We can't let him see it!"

"Oh, right," says Jess, backing up to the tall velvet drapes. "Did you *know* they were coming?"

"Of course not! You think I've got a death wish?" I snap at her.

"Sorry," Jess says. "So do I need to stand here all night, or what?"

"You could get a tail transplant," Jason says.

I can't believe my bad luck. This must be the "big social event" Dad didn't want to attend after dinner. Why didn't I ask them more questions? I thought it was some office party of Fay's — I was picturing real estate agents bobbing for apples.

One thing is for sure: If Dad and Fay recognize me half as quickly as Adam did, I'll be grounded for *life*. I desperately need to stay out of their way.

I flip open my phone and look at the time. "How long till my mom gets here?" Jess asks.

"Half an hour."

"I'm sorry, that's too long to stand with my butt in the

curtains. That tablecloth's buried in sequins and mesh." Jess steps forward. "But you've got to get yourself out of this ballroom, and pronto."

She's right. The longer I stay here, the more chance of Dad and Fay seeing me. It's only a matter of time.

I can feel my palms sweating. I've been in some really close spots before, but never like this. The Fay factor adds new dimensions of terror.

I take another sneak peek as their foursome approaches the hot buffet table. Fay puts her hands on her hips, and I can imagine her saying, "Can you believe all this free food when we just paid for dinner?"

Maid Marian shrugs and picks up a small plate. *Why not*, she appears to be saying. *It's free.*

They've all got their backs to the dance floor while they're checking out the buffet, so this seems like a safe time to scoot out the door. I don't have a clue what I'll do after that — hope Amelia is somewhere nearby? Follow Will out to the parking lot? Spend half an hour in the ladies' lounge? — but I'm getting out while the getting is good.

I walk out past the guy wearing the turban, and notice him checking my wrist to make sure I'm legit. My bracelet is right where it should be, and I just hope his memory isn't so sharp that he realizes that he never put one on me. But he doesn't say anything, and I breathe a sigh of relief as soon as I'm out of the ballroom.

And then I get my first stroke of good luck all evening (other than getting to come in the first place, of course!): Amelia is taking a shift in the coat check room.

"Boy, am I glad to see *you*!" I say.

"Ditto." She opens the half door in the counter to let me in, clearly glad to have company. "Everybody who's planning to come to this thing is already here, and most people aren't going to leave until after the show, so it's a wide world of boring right now."

"I could do with some boring," I tell her. "You see those two coats?" Pointing at Dad's old gray tweed and Fay's fur-collared car coat, I breathlessly tell her the whole story.

"So you mean you're supposed to be grounded, right now?" says Amelia. "And you came here instead? That's pretty hard-core. I'm impressed."

"Look who's talking, Ms. Stadium Crasher. Did you see if Will went outside?"

She shakes her head. "I've been sitting here counting the stripes on that scarf. It's a total snooze."

Sounds *perfect*. But snoozing is not in the cards for me. As soon as I sit on the wooden stool next to Amelia's, I realize I've drunk too much soda tonight. "Where is the ladies'?" I ask, and she points down the hall.

I scurry off to the ladies' lounge and rush inside. And there, coming out of a stall in her red-and-gold shepherdess costume, is Kayleigh.

I take a deep breath. It's like some sort of contest: Who's going to be the first person to recognize me — Kayleigh, Dad, or Fay?

But Kayleigh just gushes, "Hi, Taylor," with a really warm smile she would never give me as Diana. "OMG, Adam is *so dreamy*! And such an incredible dancer!"

She's right about that.

"Did you really do shows together at drama camp?" Kayleigh asks, sounding so eager that it's almost sweet.

If Adam says so, then I guess we did. I know his *Playbill* bio backward and forward, so I could pull out any one of his credits, but I pick one that's sure to let her do the talking. "We were in *Our Town*."

"No way! *I* just played Emily Webb in *Our Town*! That was how I got together with Ethan — he played George Gibbs. And that other girl, Jess, was my mother!"

"Really," I say, dripping Taylor disinterest. "I'm sure she was great."

"She's really talented," Kayleigh says, and I blink. It's the last thing on earth I'd expect her to say, and it makes me wonder if maybe she isn't as mean as I think. But Taylor's not softening, even if I am.

"Excuse me," I say, pushing past her.

"Small world, huh?" Kayleigh says as I enter a stall.

She has no idea *how* small.

Chapter Ten

When I get back to the coat check, Amelia is standing behind the half door with her cell in one hand. "They just announced the Fleet Feet dancers inside," she tells me. "I have to go watch my sister or Mom's going to freak. Do you want to hang out here, or should I get one of the volunteers?"

"I'll stay right here," I tell her. "It's safer." She nods and we change places. As Amelia goes in through the ballroom door, I hear the familiar strains of Tchaikovsky's "Waltz of the Snowflakes" inside.

I sit on the stool, trying to picture the ballerinas in their pale blue tutus and toe shoes, arching their graceful arms. When I was little, my parents got me all dressed up in a poufy pink party dress and took me to see *Swan Lake* at Lincoln Center. I'd never been in a building so big, and it scared me at first. But as soon as the curtain came up on Prince Siegfried's birthday ball, I was entranced. For weeks and weeks after, I dreamed about flocks of swans in blue moonlight, and acted out scenes with my teddy bear playing the evil magician.

I hear two male voices approaching and I look up. Not a moment too soon: The two men are the Robin Hood guy . . . and my *father*. And they're heading right for the coat check!

Instinctively I drop to the floor, ducking behind the half door and scuttling on hands and knees to the corner where no one can see me. I can hear their two voices approaching.

"I just want to check in," Dad is saying. My heart's pounding out of control as I bunch myself into a ball, pulling Jason's cape over my head. Under cover and hoping the sound will be muffled, I whip out my cell and start frantically texting, my thumbs in a blur:

HELP!!!! dad at coat check

I send it to Amelia and hold my breath. What if she turned her phone off? If they lean over the customer counter and see me, my life will be over.

They've reached the half door. "Anyone in there?" Dad calls out. "Hello?"

"Maybe they're way in the back," Robin Hood says. He dings on the counter bell next to the tip jar. "Hello?"

"That's strange," says Dad. "There was a blond girl working here a few minutes ago. Maybe she went to the bathroom."

"You see your coat anywhere?" Robin Hood jokes. "We could just help ourselves. Help ourselves to the tip jar, too."

I'm practically fainting when I hear Amelia's voice bustling toward us. "Sorry! I went in to watch the show," she says, opening the half door and coming inside. Of course she spots me in the corner, but she turns to the counter, all business. "So what can I do for you gentlemen?"

Dad hands her his claim check tag. "I just need my coat for a moment. I left my phone in the pocket."

And then it hits me. Oh, no! He's about to call *me*!

158

Amelia takes the tag and goes to the back of the closet, fetching his coat. As she hands it to Dad, she says, "You'll get better reception outside."

She's my hero!

"Thanks," says Dad. As he and Robin Hood head for the revolving door, I can hear him saying, "I know it sounds nuts, but she's only thirteen."

"I remember it like it was yesterday," says Robin Hood.

The second they're out of sight, Amelia turns to me, gesturing. "Put it on vibrate so it won't ring!"

I do, not a moment too soon. My phone shakes in my hand. I let it go two or three times, then answer in the sleepiest voice I can muster, ". . . Hello?"

Amelia flashes a thumbs-up.

"Oh, no, did I wake you?" says Dad.

"No . . . yes. I guess so," I mumble. "Where are you?"

"Go back to sleep. We'll be home in an hour."

"Okay," I say sleepily. "Night-night."

I hang up, and Amelia says, "Brilliant!"

"You saved my li —" I start, but she holds a finger up to her lips and turns back to the counter.

"Wow, that was *quick*!" she says with a bright smile as Dad hands back his coat.

"Thank you," he says. "Much obliged." And he takes out his wallet and puts a five-dollar bill into the tip jar.

There's a burst of applause from inside the ballroom as Dad and the Robin Hood guy go back through the door. An amplified voice says, "The Fleet Feet Dancers! Don't miss our holiday *Nutcracker*!"

I look at Amelia. "I'm really sorry you missed Zoe's dance."

"Please, I've sat through a million rehearsals. That was *close*!"

"Tell me about it," I say, standing up. "I just panicked. I mean, Dad was three feet away, there was no way that he wouldn't know who I was. So I hit the floor."

"Turn around," says Amelia. "Whoa, that floor is *dusty*!" I turn, and she brushes off Jason's cape. We hear more music coming from inside the ballroom: the guest stars from *Bye Bye Birdie*, singing "The Telephone Hour."

How appropriate.

"Do you want to go see that?" I ask Amelia. "Dad thinks I'm asleep in my bed; he won't call me again."

"I'll pass," she says. "You?"

I shake my head. "I'm just trying to get through the next twenty minutes without getting caught."

"Sounds like a plan," says Amelia, and we sit side by side in the coat check room, listening to the number from *Birdie*. As my heartbeat slows back down to normal, I wonder where Will is right now. Did he really walk out of the building? Why would he do that, except . . . could he really be *jealous*? Even though we're not officially going out? It's hard to imagine, but boys are a different species. If I think about it, it's almost a little bit flattering.

Not that there's any reason for Will to be jealous of Adam. He's drop-dead gorgeous, of course, and I do have a crush on him (how could I not?), but the sad truth is, he isn't into me that way at all. He's four years and seven months older than me (of course I know just when his birthday is), and besides that, he's *famous*. He's been on TV, he's the star of a Broadway show, he's got fan sites on YouTube and Facebook, and he's . . .

He's performing! The telephone number from *Birdie* is over, and I'd know that music cue anyway. It's the intro to Adam and Sigrid's love ballad from *Angel*. I hear the first words in his beautiful voice and melt into a puddle.

"Is that your friend Adam?" Amelia says. "Wow, he can *sing*."

No kidding! And dance, and act, and . . . I have to go watch this.

"Maybe if we stand right next to the door . . ." I say.

"Sure," says Amelia. "They're all looking at the stage anyway, right?" So we go to the edge of the door, and I peek in, scanning the room for Dad and Fay. They're still near the buffet with their friends, and they're facing the stage, with their backs to me. Phew!

We stand next to the turban guy, gazing at Adam and Sigrid. They've taken their masks off, and look into each other's eyes as their wonderful voices rise upward and intertwine. How could I not fall a little in love?

Especially when I'm remembering going to opening night, and the great party afterward, and going out into the twinkle-lit garden and dancing with him in the moonlight. It sounds like a scene from a movie, but it really happened. To *me*.

I'm so caught up in my memories and the romantic duet that I feel like I'm somewhere up high in that starlit sky, floating with Adam. When the ballad is over and everyone's clapping and cheering, I don't do the sensible thing and dodge right back into the coat check room. I stand clapping and cheering with everyone else, watching Adam and Sigrid take bow after bow. Even when that Zaloom guy comes back to the mike, I stand rooted in place, like my feet have grown into the floor. *If I could make music like that with somebody*, I'm thinking, *I wouldn't need anything else.*

What is he saying? A dance contest. Each of the stars will pick out somebody to . . . Adam is first. There's a squeal and clamor of female voices as girls wave their hands. I see Kayleigh and Jess shoot their hands in the air, but Adam is looking around the room, shielding his eyes, until he spots . . .

Me.

I shake my head violently, but it's too late. There's no way to escape. Adam's pointing and smiling, beckoning to me to join him, and everyone's turning to look, and a spotlight is swiveling, and . . .

I. Am. So. Dead.

"Go!" whispers Turban Guy. "He's pointing at *you*!"

I want to sink right through the floor, but that isn't an option. *What would Taylor do?* I ask myself, and the answer is simple. She'd draw herself up to her two inches taller than Diana height and stride through the crowd as if she completely deserved this. I head toward the stage, praying my mask, high heels, and attitude are enough to disguise me. Through the left eyehole of my mask, I can see Fay and Dad and the Robin Hoods near the chocolate fountain, and make sure to stand on the stage so my back is to all of them. That means that I'm facing my friends. Jess and Jason look just as panicked as I feel myself. Ethan's with them, but Kayleigh is not.

Sigrid is picking her dance partner now, and the *Bye Bye Birdie* cast heads into the audience, each of them grabbing someone by the hand and leading them back through the rustling, excited crowd. The celebrity judges are Mikhail Zaloom and Amelia's mother.

We line up in pairs for the contest, and I whisper urgently, "Adam, I have to lose."

"What? Why?" he whispers back.

164

"My dad and stepmother are standing behind me."

"And you're not supposed to be here?" Adam guesses.

I nod. "My stepmother will go ballistic if she recognizes me. Please help me."

"Is everyone ready?" booms the ballet master, raising his hands to cue a technician. The music comes on. It's a waltz.

How perfect is that? I learned how to waltz when I was in *My Fair Lady*, and Adam's a pro. We could so win this contest, but the longer I stay on this dance floor, the more chance I'll be caught. I have to think of a way to get out of here, and fast.

"Trip me," I whisper in Adam's ear.

"What?" He looks startled.

"Just do it. I won't —"

Adam's leg flips in front of me and I go flying. And so does my mask.

"Are you all right?" Adam gasps as I sprawl on the floor. "I'm so sorry!"

I can't tell if he's acting or not, but everyone's staring at us. "Are you hurt?" someone asks, and "Do you need a doctor?"

"I'm *fine*," I say, keeping my head down as I scramble for my mask on hands and knees. Adam waves his arms to keep people's attention on him.

"She's all right. Keep dancing," he says. "Not to worry."

Not to *worry*? Fat chance!

My right ankle is throbbing a little, but much worse than that, I can see the skirt of Fay's violet dress dead ahead. If I lift my head up, she'll have a clear view of my face.

But my floor-level view takes in something else: a pair of black cowboy boots hurrying toward me. It's Will!

Without missing a beat, he grabs a white linen napkin off the buffet table, scoops it full of ice cubes, and squats down beside me. "Cover your face," he whispers. "They'll think it's for bruises." I obey gladly, holding the wet napkin over my eyes as he helps me back up to my feet. Meanwhile Amelia, Jess, Jason, and Ethan come flying from all sides to help me.

"Get Taylor some Tylenol," Jason says loudly. Amelia says, "First aid kit right down the hall," as Ethan and Jess go to rescue my mask.

166

Between them, Will, and Adam, I'm completely hidden from Fay's prying eyes as my wonderful friends form a cluster around me, leading me out through the side door behind the buffet.

"I am so sorry," Adam keeps saying as my friends hustle me down the hall. "I just meant to make you stumble in front of the judges, not go sprawling."

"It's fine," I say. "Honest."

"You're really not hurt?" Will asks, pulling off the wet towel.

"Well, my face is a little bit frozen, but hey, it worked. Thank you so much," I say. "All of you."

"You're hobbling," says Jess.

"I'm *fine*. I think maybe I broke your mom's shoe."

"No biggie. She's not going to wear them again anyway."

I look back at Will, who's taken his mask off. It's the first time our faces have been completely uncovered all night.

"Where did you *come* from?" I ask him.

"That storeroom," he says, looking very embarrassed.

"I was going to walk home, but I realized Jess's mom would be coming and no one would know where I was. I just needed . . . to get some air. Know what I mean?"

I do know. And I'm really grateful to him, just for being himself. I look over at Adam. Adam Kessler the star, who looks totally out of place here in the hall with my middle school friends. "You better get back to the contest," I tell him.

"I don't think I'll win it," he says with a rueful smile. "Tripping your dance partner is kind of a deal breaker."

"Even so. You've got an audience."

Adam nods, looking at me with those gorgeous blue eyes. My heart rises into my throat. Is he going to hug me good-bye? I think I'd completely dissolve. I can feel Will watching the two of us.

"Great to see you again, Diana," Adam finally says. "You're a really good actress." And he reaches out for my hand and gives it a big-brotherly squeeze.

A really good actress. Did he really say that? So much for heaven on earth, I think wistfully as I watch Adam Kessler walk down the hall, heading back into the ballroom. I'll just have to make do with earth on earth.

I look at my friends. I'm surrounded by people who care about me — by Jess and Jason, Amelia, and Ethan, and best of all, quick-thinking Will, who just saved the day with that napkin trick. He's not looking over my shoulder the way that he did on the dance floor. He's looking right into my eyes.

Jess's cell phone trills with a text, and she looks at the screen. "Talk about timing," she says. "My mom's in the parking lot."

I ask Jess's mom to drop me back at my house in my ball gown — I don't dare take the time to go back to Jess's and change. The benefit runs until midnight, but I know my dad, and I'm guessing he got Fay to leave the second the dance contest was over. Which means they could arrive home any minute.

I rush inside, where my homework arrangement is still sitting there on the dining table. As I dash up the stairs, I don't even bother to take off the wobbly high heels. My ankle's a little sore, but the last thing I want to do is get caught downstairs in this dress.

I snap on my night-light, but leave off the overhead

light in my bedroom, which someone might see through my window. Then I peel off my evening gloves, unzip the pink gown, and stuff it into a big laundry bag with the mask and the broken shoes — I'll deal with all that stuff tomorrow.

I have just enough time to pull on my pajamas and jump under the covers before I hear Fay's SUV pulling into the driveway below. My heart pounds at the thought of how close I just came to a total disaster. I'm home, and I'm safe.

What a night!

Chapter Eleven

The doorbell rings way too early on Saturday morning, or maybe it's just that I stayed up too late at the masquerade ball. One way or another, I'm really not ready to greet trick-or-treaters at ten in the morning.

Dad's taking a shower and Fay is still wearing her bathrobe, so I'm the one who gets sent to the door with a basket of Kit Kat bars left from the cleaners. My ankle's still a bit sore, but I try not to limp. I don't want Fay asking me how it got twisted. I'm just lucky I didn't sprain it, or worse.

I pull open the front door, expecting to see a few neighborhood toddlers in spangled tights with their moms. But no — it's my stepsisters.

"What are you doing back here already?" I ask, startled to see them. "I thought you were all going trick-or-treating with Marissa today."

"We *would*," Ashley says, "if Mom hadn't forgotten our costumes."

"Oh, for goodness' sake," says Fay, coming to join us. "They were right in the hall, where your sleeping bags were. Do I have to take care of everything?"

"You're the *mom*," Ashley says in a voice that means duh, yes, of course. Brynna snatches a Kit Kat bar out of the bowl.

"Did Marissa's mom drive you all the way over?" asks Fay. "She could have just called me."

"She tried, but she says our phone's broken," says Brynna.

Oops. That's one thing I didn't remember to put back to normal last night.

"I'll have to go thank her," Fay says, pulling her coat over her bathrobe. "Grab the costume bag, Brynna. And don't eat that candy. I'm sure you've already had plenty of sugar."

"It's *Halloween*!" Brynna whines, but she picks up the bag with their costumes inside. All three of them tromp out the door, and I see Fay go up to the idling car as Marissa's mom lowers the driver's side window to speak with her.

I look back at the bowl of Kit Kats in my hand and remember I'm grounded. It *is* Halloween, and I'm going to spend all day answering that doorbell while my friends get dressed up and go trick-or-treating.

Well, I had enough fun and excitement last night to last me a while. If I don't get to put on a costume today, I'll survive.

But then I imagine the Vampire Prom Queens without me, and feel a sharp pang about having to miss all the fun. Especially since we're all starting high school next year, and who knows how much longer we'll feel young enough to dress up in costumes and go around asking for candy. I can't imagine ever outgrowing it, but people do. Amelia told me that Zoe and her friends are going out to the movies tonight, and Will's big brother Steve and his band are rehearsing. On Halloween!

Dad comes downstairs fully dressed, with his hair still wet from the shower. "Good morning," he says. "Boy, we all overslept."

I go over to kiss him, enjoying the shaving cream smell. "Did you have fun last night?" I ask, avoiding his gaze.

"Well, you know." He shrugs. "It's more Fay's thing than mine, but yes, I did have a good time. Except for the missing my daughter part. How about you? Were you lonesome?"

"Not at *all*," I say, glad to be able to tell him the truth about something.

"Where's Fay?" asks Dad, helping himself to a cup of black coffee. "Did somebody come to the door? I thought I heard the doorbell."

Before I can answer, Fay comes back inside, peeling off her coat. "Well, that was embarrassing. Alison Lane had to drive all the way over here to pick up the girls' costumes. What's wrong with that phone?"

"Maybe the battery's dead," says Dad. "It wasn't working last night either."

Fay strides into the kitchen and sees the handset lying on its side next to the dish drainer. She picks it up, turning toward me. "Did you do this, Diana?"

"I don't know," I say, acting confused. "I guess maybe when I made my dinner. I didn't notice, but . . ."

"You didn't notice." Fay puts the phone back in the handset, shooting Dad a you-see? look.

I'm still grounded, for sure. There's no point even asking if she'll change her mind. I go into the dining room, planning to clear off the table for breakfast. As I start removing the research books and colored pencils, Dad comes up from behind with his coffee cup. He picks up the brochure, smiling at the French flag letters on the front cover.

He sits down and starts leafing through it. "You did a marvelous job on this, honey. It's really creative."

"Thanks," I say. I sneak a look over at Fay, but her frown stays in place. So that's it, then. All that extra work I did didn't make any difference at all. I'm going to be stuck home all weekend.

Somehow I choke down my cereal and toast and go back to my bedroom. I keep trying to tell myself not to be too disappointed, but that never works. I *am* disappointed. There's no use pretending I'm not.

I flip open my laptop, and there's Adam Kessler's face, smiling at me. I still can't believe that I actually *saw* him last night. Talked to him. *Danced* with him. There's something strange, though: I don't feel the same bubbly heart flutter that I felt last night. When I look at his photo now, in the clear light of day, Adam isn't some fantasy dreamboat who makes my heart flip-flop. He's just a cute guy.

Who can sing, dance, and act.

And trip people on cue.

I bend over to rub my right ankle, then type a quick post to Jess:

still grounded :(

Jess answers right away:

so stinks!

She's got that right.

Our friends are meeting at Jess's house at five o'clock to get dressed for the evening, and they're all trading messages like crazy on Facebook. Sara tells everyone that she's going to be wearing her grandmother's sari and candy-wax vampire fangs, which she bought at the Underhill Deli.

They're awesome. I can't wait!

I smile. Sara must be the only thirteen-year-old girl on the planet who uses capital letters and correct punctuation on all of her posts and text messages. The Spelling Bee champ in her just can't resist.

Amelia can, though. Her message reads:

me 2 bff c u there

This is making me sad. I shut my laptop and go back downstairs, where I do chores and clean house for the next several hours without saying a word, except when the doorbell rings and I troop to the door to greet some pint-size fairy princess or ninja. It's fun seeing what different kids choose to wear — it's like getting a glimpse of their most secret selves.

I'm in the kitchen refilling the basket of Kit Kats when Dad comes in for his afternoon decaf and cookies.

"I'm sorry," he says, getting milk from the fridge.

"Sorry for what?" I ask him.

"For making you stay home this evening. On Halloween. I know how much you love getting dressed up."

That's right, Dad. If only he knew.

He watches me empty the Kit Kat bag into the basket before he goes on. "You've been working and working all day, and you did a great job on your project for French. And you haven't complained or tried lobbying to change my mind. I appreciate that."

I look at him. "So . . . does that mean you'll let me go out with my friends?"

Dad shakes his head. "I can't do that, Diana. Actions have consequences. And you need to know that Fay and I mean what we say."

Oh, I know that, all right. "I understand," I say, and the truth is, I do. I know taking that tablecloth wasn't the right thing to do. Neither was sneaking out of the house and into the Hunger Unmasked Ball last night. But I'm so glad I did.

The doorbell rings, and I pick up my basket of Kit Kats and head for the door. When I open it, though, there's nobody there. I scan up and down the street, mystified. It's almost dark, and there's a hint of red on the horizon. Perfect Halloween lighting. If this was a stage set, it couldn't be better. Then I hear a bush giggle.

I circle around it, and there are my friends!

"Trick or treat!" they all shout, cracking up.

"Total treat," I say. "Get out from behind that forsythia. I want to see you."

The Vampire Prom Queens look fabulous. Jess and Amelia are wearing their gowns from last night, plus tiaras and fangs and the beauty queen sashes that Nelson made. Sara is draped in a bright crimson sari that matches the blood on her wax-candy fangs. They've made themselves up really pale, with a lot of mascara and eyeliner. I would have so loved to be part of this act, but I don't want to pout.

"You guys *rock*!" I exclaim, holding out the full basket of Kit Kats. They all plunge their hands in.

"I'm so sorry you're grounded," says Sara. "That totally stinks."

"It totally does," I say. "Where are the guys?"

"Look behind you," says Jess.

I turn around as Will steps out from behind the bush on the opposite side. He's wearing his father's maroon rocker tux, with his hair slicked back Dracula-style. I don't think I've ever seen his forehead before.

"You make a great vampire," I tell him.

"I should've stuck with Kurt Cobain," he mumbles through fake plastic fangs. Ethan emerges right next to him, wearing a black cape and glittery Robert Pattinson–style makeup, but Kayleigh is nowhere in sight.

"No clown suit tonight?" I ask as I hand him a Kit Kat. "And where's Kayleigh?"

"Kayleigh who, Tayloraylor?" says Ethan. "Oh, you must mean my ex."

"You broke up?" I say gleefully as Jess shouts, "Your EX?"

"You heard it here first," Ethan says.

"So you finally came to your senses and ditched her? You did something *right*?" says Jess.

"When?" Sara asks.

"Last night at the Hunger Unmasked Ball."

"Ooh, harsh," grins Amelia.

"Hey," says Ethan. "She was all over that Adam guy. You don't dis the Horowitz."

"Aka Bozo," says Jess.

"Aka free man and glad of it, fish tail. Where is *Jason* today?"

"They've got some dorm party thing at the Foreman Academy," Jess says.

"Fancy schmantzy," says Ethan.

"That must be so weird, spending holidays at your school," Sara shudders.

"That place is creepy," says Will. "I like Weehawken Middle School better."

So do I, I think, looking at him. All around us are costumed kids clutching pumpkin-shaped buckets, running gleefully over their neighbors' lawns with their parents behind them. A lot of the houses are decorated with skeletons, carved jack-o'-lanterns, and flickering candles.

"Who wants to go score some more candy?" asks Ethan.

"Drowning your sorrows in sugar," says Jess. "So sad."

Ethan elbows her in the ribs, and she slaps him back playfully. As they walk ahead, flanked by Amelia and Sara, Will says, "I'll catch up with you guys in a minute, okay?"

"Sure thing," says Jess. "Bye, Diana." She's smiling a lot.

Will turns back so we're facing each other. "That was fun last night," he says.

"It was wonderful," I agree. "Even the scary parts."

"Is your ankle okay?"

"It's fine. It was nothing."

Will nods. "That's good." He clears his throat. "Sorry I acted so weird about, you know, that actor guy."

"You didn't act weird," I assure him.

"Yeah, I did, but I'm over it now. Famous people are . . . I don't know, different."

I know what he means. It's as if there's more light in the room when you're with them, but it's just the glow of your own dreams. I look at Will. We're standing in front of the hedge that divides our front yard from the Wheelers', and they've twined its branches with twinkling orange lights.

"I brought something for you," Will mumbles.

"Really?" I'm very surprised. And pleased.

Will reaches down into his trick-or-treat bag and takes out a smaller bag. "Here," he says, giving it to me. His hand bumps against mine. It's like an electric shock.

I look inside the bag, which is chock-full of Halloween candy.

"I knew you couldn't go out, so I've been getting doubles at every house," Will explains.

"That's so nice of you. Thanks." Am I blushing? I think so.

In fact, I'm pretty sure.

"There's some Mentos," Will says, reaching out for the bag. His hand bumps against mine again. Just as I'm

182

thinking *This can't be an accident*, I feel his fingers twine through mine. We're holding hands.

I'm standing in front of a hedge full of pinpoints of light, holding hands with Will Carson. The reflected lights shine like stars in his eyes.

And there, in a flash, is that same delicious heart flutter I missed when I looked at the photo of Adam this morning. It didn't go away after all, I realize, flooding with joy as Will gives my hand a quick squeeze. It just took off its mask.

Don't miss

#5: Scheme Spirit

There are only two people at Cinderella Cleaners who don't like me, and today they're standing side by side at the counter. My supervisor, Miss MacInerny, is at the cash register and Lara is working the conveyor belt's foot pedal, keeping her eye on the clothes swishing past in their clear plastic bags. Neither one of them greets me, so I walk past them to Dad's office.

His door is open, and as always, his whole face lights

up when he sees me. He gets up from his desk chair and gives me a hug. "How was school?" he asks.

"Fine." I hesitate. I want to ask about getting to act in the production of *The Snow Queen*, but I'm still on probation for making a mermaid tail out of that tablecloth. What if Dad thinks I'm not committed enough to keep working here? A few months ago, I would have leapt at the chance to quit my after-school job and go back to Drama full-time, but I've fallen in love with the cleaners. I've made some great friends, and it's opened the door to so many amazing adventures. The truth is, I'd miss it like crazy if I had to leave.

"What is it?" he asks.

I could say something bland about the weather, but he'd see right through it. Besides, it's a chance to be part of the holiday show! So I tell him what Ms. Wyant said.

"It's a *solo*," I say, my voice lifting with breathless excitement. I can practically feel my eyes shining.

Dad looks me over, considering it. "The holiday season's our busiest time," he says. "From Thanksgiving to Christmas, it all just explodes. Winter coats, party clothes, seasonal businesses . . . and I'm sure you remember that you need to pay for replacing that tablecloth." I nod, disappointed. Why did I think he'd say yes?

But Dad isn't done yet. "I'll tell you what, though. I could use some more hands on these next busy weekends. You said that Ms. Wyant will need you for five days during — what is it called again, tech week? So let's make a trade. I'll give you those five afternoons off if you'll come in to work for the next five Saturdays."

"Dad, that's fantastic!" I say, moving to hug him. And then I remember. The Homecoming game!

"Something wrong?" he says, reading my change of expression.

"Not exactly . . . It's just that this Saturday's Homecoming, and I've already made plans to go with my friends."

Dad raises his eyebrows. I'm afraid he's going to tell me that I'm trying to have my cake and eat it, too, or one of those other parent clichés. But he just says mildly, "Well, then, you've got a decision to make. Which is more important to you?"

The holiday show or the Homecoming game? How can I choose?